Time Pocket

Written by Erin M Courtney

Erin M Courtney

*In Loving Memory
of My Aunt Linda*

Part One

Chapter 1

Piper 1819

Mist lingered over "Little Plantation" and the outskirts of New Orleans. Piper loved celebrations on her birthday August 3, 1819, and this particular party was going to change her life forever.

The Little Plantation was in all its glory on this day, the perfect setting for Piper's party. Early morning, Piper walked around to see that the ballroom is in her favorite colors teal and brown. The staff at the Little Plantation used the wood pillar for the brown, teal fabric around each pillar.

Now late afternoon Piper May Little 5 feet tall with her caramel-like hair and deep dark chocolate eyes. Wearing the midnight blue satin dress with a white sash, picked out by Tyler.

Meeting Tyler again tonight one year ago, and re-membering thinking what a good looking man he was.

Having to wait for all of her guests to arrive before she could go down to the ballroom. Not a very patient girl, she was walking around her room, thinking about her life, hoping she might see her childhood friend Millie again. The last time Piper had seen Millie was on Piper's 12th birthday.

Eventually, her father came and escorted her to the ballroom. All eyes were on Piper as she entered the room. Piper looked around the ball-room. As her eyes met Tyler's, she was pleased to find him wearing teal silk shirts, with a brown vest and light brown trousers. Tyler Christopher Williams 6 feet tall blonde hair and his sky blue eyes, tan kissed skin from his years working on ship. She was very happy to see he was just as good looking as she remembered. Maybe more.

First, dinner was held in their grand dining room. Piper and her family were seated and much to her amazement, Tyler sat next to her. As he sat down, his hand touched hers. Piper felt a little electricity from him and blushed. Tyler looked at her and smiled.

With dinner concluded they walked into the ballroom. Tyler asked her to dance. Tyler took Piper hand in a smooth way she thrilled by his charming style. Getting to the middle of the dance floor.

Tyler murmured, "This is not the first time we have met."

"At the town meeting a year ago."

He smiled. "And you were in a midnight blue dress that night."

"Is this why you picked this dress for me tonight?"

Tyler, with a smile upon his face, spoke, "Maybe I did, and you look stunning Piper."

The song was over. As the next one started, Tyler suggested,

"Shall we go outside for a walk, Piper?"

"I'd like that very much, sir."

"You can call me Tyler."

"I can do that, Tyler" Piper remarked, with a big smile on her face.

∞∞∞

They walked outside in the courtyard lamp lit and water fountain with lily pads, and red, orange, and yellow roses, and patch of lavender. Piper looked at Tyler. His blonde hair and wonderful smile took her breath away. His eyes were blue, like the sky. The one thing that Piper truly liked the most about Tyler was the way he talked to her with a deep gentle sweet tone. It made her feel very safe.

Tyler had been waiting for this moment alone with her all night. The dress he had picked out for her made her even more beautiful than the first time he saw her over a year ago.

"What are you thinking about Tyler?"

Tyler looked at her as he smiled.

"I'm thinking about what a perfect night this is for a walk with you."

"Thank you, Tyler. Why did you ask me out here?"

He got so close to her and whispered in her ear.

"Since all eyes are on you and me, I want to wish you a happy birthday, just the two of us."

Piper looked up at Tyler, and red in the face, not knowing what to say to him.

"Piper, I know it is hard for you not having the choice on who you want to marry."

"I wish to get to know you better, Tyler."

"As I do, Piper."

Tyler took Piper's hand in his and kissed it. Piper blushed.

"We should get back to the party before my father comes out looking for me."

Tyler still held Piper's hand, and they walked back into the ballroom. All eyes were on them again as they entered the room. Piper's mother, Kitty Roes, came up to them.

"Piper, I have something for you. Come with me."

She let go of Tyler's hand and walked with your mother up the stairs.

Piper and her mother climbed the stairs to Piper's room.

"Happy birthday, my sweet girl. I hope you like it."

Piper saw a big box on her bed. She walked over to the box. As Piper unwrapped her gift, she pulled out an astonishingly beautiful teal and white wedding dress.

"I love it!" she exclaimed as she hugged her mother.

She knew she had to be happy about the dress and getting married to someone she didn't know. That was the world she lived in. She could see sharing her life with Tyler.

"Let's get back to your party. Tyler has something for you, also."

They walked back to the ballroom. Again, everyone's eyes followed her. She found Tyler standing in the middle of the dance floor. Piper approached him and time stopped.

Millie 1999

The last time Millie Ann Brown was in the Little Plantation was on August 3, 1985, on her fifth birthday. Millie was 19 today (Aug. 3, 1999). Millie 5'7" with her red-brown hair and blue with a little bit of green eyes walked up the street pasting quite old Willow tree that had the initials of "MH + JW 1835", to Little Plantation with the big oak around the very old path, wishes that her mother Penelope Brown was still alive. Penelope had died from breast cancer the year prior.

The Little Plantation had been closed since November 1985 and re-opened in October 1996, named The Old Little Plantation. Millie was starting her first day at her new job. Millie loved history and living down the street from the Old Little Plantation. She had wanted to work at the Plantation since she was 16. As Millie walked up the white wood steps, and she opened the big front door of the house, and a wave of energy hit her. Millie saw both the new and the old, at the same time, within the plantation walls.

" Are you okay?" said Beth Green

Millie looked up at a 5'6" strawberry blonde hair crystal blue eye's woman.

" I am sorry. I forgot how amazing this place is, and the last time I was here I was only 5."

" You are Millie, the historian?"

" Yes, I am and you are Beth right?" Beth smiled at Millie.

" Yes. The last time I checked." They both laughed. Millie blushed.

Millie had learned a lot about the Little Plantation and its history since she had met Piper Little. She had looked up most of the history of The Little Plantation at the age of 12. Millie still wanted to know more about Piper Little and the home she had lived in.

" Welcome to the Old Little Plantation."

" Didn't Piper Little live here?"

" The only Piper May Little that lived in the plantation died in 1880."

" I met a Piper May Little in 1985 and she was 5 like me."

" Maybe as an actor played Piper Little for a reenactment?"

"Maybe."

Beth gave Millie a tour of the Old Little Plantation.

" I see today is your birthday."

" Yes, it is. I am 19 years old."

" I am 23 and I have been working here since I was 18."

As Millie said the words she glanced at the portrait of 5-year-old Piper.

"That's her right there. The Piper Little I met at 5."

" Are you sure?"

" Yes, I am sure."

Millie walked down the hall envisioning Piper Little growing up before her eyes. Millie got to 1819 portrait and saw the room change and then Beth was gone.

"Millie, is that you?" a voice came from behind her. Millie saw Piper Little in a midnight blue dress.

"Yes!" Piper hugged Millie.

" Happy Birthday, Millie! The last time I saw you, you were a little older."

" Last time I saw you I was 5. Happy Birthday,

Piper."

" Tonight is my coming out party, and Tyler just asked me to marry him."

Just as Millie was going to say something, Piper was gone and Beth was back.

" There you are. I was talking to you and you disappeared."

" I think I was in 1819 at Piper Little's coming-out party!"

" The stories are true then, that someone from this time can go back to Piper Little's birthday, and other times in her life. Piper has a note-book she wrote every time she met you in her timeline." She mentions a girl called "Millie Ann Brown."

Chapter 2

Piper 1819

I t was a month after Piper's birthday. Piper and Tyler were together every day after their engagement that night. Piper was over the moon seeing Millie again. Millie was 19, not older than 40. Piper writes in her notebook about Millie. She was not ready to tell Tyler about Millie yet, starting to fall in love with Tyler. Never thought she would feel this way about someone that her mother and father picked out for her.

Tyler was taking Piper out for the day on a carriage ride around town, to his favorite spot by the river. Tyler got out and helped her down from the carriage. Stephen, the carriage driver, and Piper's female companion Charlotte. Piper started to walk down to the water. Tyler watched her in a green cotton dress. Tyler set up a picnic lunch for two. Piper and Charlotte walking around, looking at the water, Piper stopped and put her feet in the water.

"Piper," Tyler said in a low and somewhat shy voice.

She turned around and saw the two sandwiches bottle of red wine and two glasses.

" Come sit down with me."

Picking up her shoes walked over and sat across from him.

When they had finished eating, Tyler got up and helped his lady up. Hand in hand they walked back to the water. Charlotte and Stephen cleaned up after them.

" Piper, you look so beautiful and I like your green dress. Did you know that green is one of my favorite colors?"

Getting a little flushed, Piper responded, "Thank you, Tyler. This spot is gorgeous."

"You are gorgeous"

He looked down at her and leaned in and kissed her. This was not their first kiss, but it was the first kiss without a crowd. She kissed him back. The kiss was everything they both wanted and more.

Out of breath, Tyler exclaimed, " That was some kiss, and nice not having everyone watching us." Tyler looked down at her "May I kiss you again?"

She just kissed him.

Loving that she just kissed him, and he kissed harder this time. Breathless and looking at each other, they kissed again.

A little time later, they started talking. The Little family was old money and the Williams family was new money. Her family had lived in the town for over 100 years. Her 2nd Great Grandfather had built the Plantation and started growing tea and other crops.

His family were ship owners and most of Tyler's life was on a ship, until he was 18. After 18, he started his own shipping business, and by the time he was 22 he was making more money than his father. Tyler started living in New Orleans around the time he first saw and met Piper at the town meeting a year ago. He got to know Sean Jack Little, her father, right after meeting her.

Piper being the oldest girl in the family. She had one older brother named Dean, 23, and two younger sisters Sara, 16, and Heather 15.

The sun started to set but they had been lost in each other. Charlotte wandered over to the two of them. Realizing it was late, Tyler walked her to the carriage. They went hand in hand to the carriage. He kissed her hand, she put her other hand on his face and kissed him.

Helping his lady out of the carriage. Stephen

the driver, took the carriage and horses back to the barn. They walked up the steps, hand in hand to the front door. Sean Jack was waiting for them.

"You are both late for dinner."

Piper went up to her room to change for dinner. Getting to her room her heart going so quickly by being with Tyler all-day. Looking at her wardrobe seeing the perfect gown forest green for the evening.

∞∞∞

After dinner, they walked around the garden still holding hands. The garden with the big glass lanterns lighting their path. Her heart was all in a flutter every time he was close to her. Tyler had lived in their guesthouse since the end of August. Tyler shared that he had lost his mother at the age of 15. Talking about his mother, hearing his story and getting to know him, she knew she was falling in love with Tyler.

She asked him if he would take her on his ship soon. He loved the idea, and he started making plans for their day out on the water. She had never been on a ship before. They planned to go on the ship after they got married in February. He walked her back up to the house for the night. He kissed her hand.

"Goodnight, my Piper." She kissed him on the cheek.

" Goodnight, Tyler. I hope to see you tomorrow."

They kissed with their eyes. She walked into the house and he walked to the guesthouse for the night.

Millie 1999

Millie had been at her new job for almost a month. Millie and Beth had started to become really close friends. Millie was still very floored every time she saw Piper. Millie had found the notebooks that Piper had written in. Seeing her name in Piper's timeline. She started looking up all she could on Piper's life. Millie was in the plantation library and many books were on The Little and The Williams families. Beth came into the room.

" Millie, your first tour is here."

They are both in period attire from 1820. Millie dressed in a French silk plum-colored dress. Beth was in an 1822 French silk green dress. Millie started the first tour of the day, and had 10 tours that day.

∞∞∞

At the end of the day, Millie went to the old ballroom. Beth went to go get them dinner. Millie was in the house by herself when the room changed on her again, into the Little's ballroom. She got up from her chair. Millie walked out of the room into the sitting room and saw a good looking man with blonde hair and blue eyes. Tyler turned around.

" Who are you?"

"I am Millie and I work here. Who are you, sir?"

" I am Tyler Williams. I am with Miss Piper, one of the ladies of the house."

"I know Piper."

Time stops.

∞∞∞

"Millie, there you are." Millie now seeing Beth

" It happened again."

"Really, did you see Piper?"

" No, Tyler Williams."

They walked back through the ballroom and into the library. Beth pulled out one of the old photo books from the Little family and pointed out a photograph of Piper Tyler's wedding.

"Is this who you met?"

Millie looked at the photograph.

"Yes, that's him"

"That is Piper's husband Tyler. They got married in November 1819."

Millie couldn't get over meeting Tyler but not seeing Piper.

Beth had been working at The Old Little Plantation for 5 years and had read all of Piper Little's notebooks about Piper meeting Millie in her time.

Millie still had no idea how she was finding time pocket.

∞∞∞

One of the days when Beth was off, Millie was looking up Piper and Tyler's life at the plantation. She loved reading about them. Beth had mentioned that there were additional notebooks but she didn't know where Beth had placed them.

After closing, Millie went up to the oldest part of the Little Plantation, the bedrooms. This area of the plantation was not part of the tour, but the staff would go to check that all was secured for the night. Millie did not know she was in Piper's room.

"Millie, is that you?" An older voice said to her.

" Yes, who is in here?" 80-year-old Piper came into the light.

" I am Piper Little."

" Piper!" Millie looked at the 80-year-old Piper, and she was in Millie's time.

" Piper, you are in the year 1999."

" No, you are in the year 1880." Millie put the light on in Piper's room. Piper looked up at the light.

" I AM in your time."

" Yes, you are." The room looked like the 1880 room with 1990's lights. Millie sat next to Piper on the bed.

Older Piper said in a sad way,

   " Millie, I miss you, my old friend"

   As Millie asked Piper about her time, Piper was suddenly gone again.

Chapter 3

Piper 1819

October was Piper's favorite month because the Little Plantation had an autumn festival each year. This year the Fall dance would be the first time Piper and Tyler would be hosting. Kitty had become like a mother to Tyler during the past two months.

Piper and her mom had started looking at the wedding planning. The wedding would be a big town event. They would use the Little Plantation courtyard for the ceremony and the ballroom for the reception. The wedding was set for February 14.

∞∞∞

Life at the Little Plantation was about to change. Sean Jack Little had been sick for the last three weeks. Kitty Little wanted to cancel the festival.

" No, this is Piper's favorite time of year," insisted Sean Jack.

"We will continue on for her, then."

It was Tyler's first time hosting a party. Piper had always hosted parties with mother and father at her side, so this was new to her. Kitty was staying upstairs with Sean.

As the party was going on downstairs, Kitty was helping Sean go through and finalize a will. Sean knew he was dying. He wanted to make sure plans were in place for his family. The Little Plantation would go to Piper and Tyler after they got married.

Unaware of how serious her father's illness was, Piper thoroughly enjoyed the autumn festival. It was everything she'd hoped for. She was so grateful that Tyler was at her side. They started dancing. She was so happy to be with him tonight. He took his lady outside to the courtyard.

Once outside, Piper looked up at the full moon. Tyler was watching her with love in his eyes.

" Piper," she looked at him.

" Yes, Tyler." He took her hand and pulled her in close.

"Piper, I am so in love with you, I can't wait for you to be my wife." He said this with a big smile on his face.

" I love you, too." His hand was under her chin and he kissed her with so much love in his heart.

Staying outside for some time they were lost in each other's eyes. Charlotte came outside to get them.

"Miss Piper." They had forgotten about the party.

"Yes, Charlotte."

"Miss Piper and Mister Tyler, the guests are starting to leave."

They walked to the front door to say goodnight to their guests. They said goodbye to everyone.

∞∞∞

Tyler went up the stairs with Piper to say good-night to Piper's parents. As they got to the door of the room, time stopped.

Millie 1999

Millie had been working at the Plantation for two months and loved her job. Millie would stay, even when her shift was over. Loved the history of the place. Millie and Beth were also getting closer. Millie had known she liked girls since she was 12. Millie had been with one other girl in high school. Millie was not sure if Beth was into her or not.

∞∞∞

One night all of that changed. They were closing the plantation together. As the last tour left and saw that Millie was alone in The Old Little Plantation, went to the desk at the front of the Plantation, and saw a note from Beth saying.

" Getting dinner for the two of us. Be back soon."

Millie got a little bit excited, going into the dining room in the Old Little Plantation, and set up the table for the two of them.

Almost done when Beth came in with the food. They sat and talked about the day. They started opening up about their life.

"Millie" Beth said nervous

" Yes Beth"

"Are you into girls?" Millie smiled at Beth.

" I am. Are you into girls also?" Beth got up from her chair and went over to Millie

" Yes I am and I really like to kiss you now."

Millie got up from her chair and looked at Beth. Millie kissed Beth and Beth kissed Millie back.

"WOW" and kissed again.

∞∞∞

The next day Millie was still on cloud 9 after kissing Beth last night. Started in the Fall event at the Old Little Plantation. Was in her office working on the Fall event. Looking at an old photograph of the Little family at Fall party. Saw something in one of the photographs for 1835, and saw herself in the background, with a very good looking man.

Chapter 4

Piper 1819

One month after Sean Jack Little had passed away. Tyler was in the house every day helping his lady with the Little Plantation. Piper's older brother came home to be with his family. Dean was not a big fan of Plantation life. Dean was more into a city life. Dean and Tyler are the same age of 23. Dean was not willing to get married yet. That's why Piper got the Little Plantation. Two younger sisters were very happy to see their big brother.

Dean and Piper looked at the books and the Will.

" looks like your wedding is getting moved up."

Wedding November 18, 1819

Piper was happy to be marrying Tyler, but also very sad that her father was not there to walk her down the aisle. Dean was staying for the wedding, and he was going to walk his little sister down the aisle.

The day of the wedding. Upstairs in her room with her mother.

" My sweet Piper I know you miss having your father here. Your father loved you and really liked Tyler. I know your father is watching over you today. I am so relieved that you and Tyler like each other." Starting to cry at her mother's words.

"I love you so much, Mommy. Tyler loves me and I love him."

Let her mother know that she and her sisters will still live at The Little Plantation with her and Tyler.

Everyone in town was at Piper and Tyler's wedding. Dean walked her down the aisle to Tyler. Piper's wedding dress was teal and white. The Sun was setting as Piper walked to Tyler. He was so happy to be marrying her. As they kissed.

They danced almost every dance. The room was in Piper and Tyler colors, teal and midnight blue, brown and white. After some time dancing, they went outside to their spot in the courtyard. He kissed her, with so much love and other feelings inside himself.

Piper and Tyler walking up the stairs to her room. As soon as the door was closed Tyler started kissing Piper.

" Tyler have you been with others like this before?" looking at her with love in his eyes.

"I have not my love." Smiled so big and kissed him.

He helped her out of her dress. He walked her back to the bed. The passion they had for each other, could set the world on fire.

November 1999

Millie had been planning a holiday dance at The Old Little Plantation and the theme will be 1819. Looked up everything she could about the little plantation parties in 1819. Millie and Beth had been seeing each other for over a month. Beth was all for the holiday dance at the Old Little Plantation.

∞∞∞

One night after closing, and it was 2 weeks before the holiday dance. They were staying the night at the house every night till the holiday event. They worked so hard to have the old little plantation look like it did in 1819. At night was the only time they could move the books out of the ballroom and into the small storage room next to Millie's room.

At 9:30 pm they take a break from cleaning. They sat down and looked at the majestic ballroom and the stories it could tell them. In the blink of the eye, the ballroom looked newer. Millie got up and so did Beth, and looked at each other.

" Are you seeing this?" Millie grabs Beth's hand.

A black man came into the ballroom and looked at them.

"Who are you?" Stephen said

"I am Millie Brown and this is Beth Green. We know Piper May Little."

"Well, Mrs. Piper Williams is up the stairs. I will get her for you."

" All books call her Piper Little," Millie said to Beth

Beth didn't know what to say. This was the first time this had happened to her.

Piper came into the ballroom with Stephen.

"MILLIE" and ran to Millie and hugged her. Piper looked at Beth.

"Millie, is this your Beth?"

"Yes, how did you know that?" Piper didn't say anything back.

Beth just stared at Piper. Beth read all of Piper notebooks over the years.

"Piper, how is Tyler doing?"

"He is doing great, but he is out on his ship right now on business for the plantation."

" What year is it?"

"It is November 1822 and I am with baby number 3."

As she said that a little boy at the age of

two came out from behind Stephen, and Stephen picked him up and walked him over to Piper.

"This is Jack Little Williams, Jack named after my father. His name was Sean Jack, and everyone called him"

"Jack."

Jack looked like his father but had his mother's eyes. Millie looked into Jack eyes and Jack

"Came home again" He looked at his mother.

Right after he said that both were gone.

It was just Millie and Beth were back in their time.

Chapter 5

December 1819

Months after Piper and Tyler got married and took care of the plantation. Piper's mother and sisters still lived in the plantation with them. The family wanted to have a holiday dance in honor of her father Sean Jack Little. Her sisters helped plan the party. Sara was 16 and 15 year old Heather. Piper other things on her mind.

Piper and her mother worked on the house as Tyler worked on the little plantation business. He knew more about the shipping business. The staff of the little plantation helped Tyler out with the plantation.

December 18 1819 a week before Christmas, Sara and Heather did a great job planning party. Piper loves everything they did for the party. This was the first event they hosted as a married couple.

This was the first time in a month that they had

fun with each other. As they were dancing, things around them changed. Piper saw Millie. Piper looked at Tyler.

"Do you see her?"

"I do." Piper started walking towards Millie. As they walked over there she disappeared. Piper and Tyler looked at each other. Went back to dancing.

They dance the night away. He looked down at his wife with so much love in his eyes and kissed her forehead. Piper looked up at him.
" I have something to tell you."

"What is it, my love?"

" I am with child." kissing her and smiling at her.

"I want to wait to tell everyone." just kissed his wife again. The room changed again.

Millie

December 18 1999 Millie and Beth both had everything up and ready to go for the holiday dance tonight. Millie and Beth were staying at the old little plantation for the past month, working on the 1819 theme dance. Just before the doors for the Old Little Plantation, both Millie and Beth saw Piper and Tyler for just a second. The energy in the little plantation was very alive tonight.

Slowly people started showing up for holiday dance. Most everyone dress in the right period attire for 1819. Millie and Beth hosting the holiday party. Beth hired a reenactor to help with the theme.

∞∞∞

Things changed as people walked into the ballroom, but only two that noticed were Millie and Beth. Piper and Tyler saw Millie and Beth again and this time they could talk together for most of the night. Millie was very happy to talk to Piper like she did at 5 years old. Millie asked Piper what year it was. Piper told her December 18, 1819. Piper told Millie all the time that she had met Millie after they were 5. Piper was 12 the next time she saw Millie but was older around the age of 40. Next time she met Millie in her timeline Millie knew that one, that was 4 months ago for Piper. Millie told Piper all the times she had seen her. Millie told her about the 2 years from now meeting.

Just before Tyler and Beth came back to Piper and Millie. Piper let Millie know she was with child. Tyler asked Piper to dance, Beth asked Millie to dance. As both Millie and Beth started to dance the room changed again, and Piper and Tyler were gone and most of the people from the time. Millie kissed Beth.

"What a night."

∞∞∞

They started cleaning up after the party. Millie sat down for little and started falling asleep.

"Millie you should go to bed. I will be up soon." Beth said to Millie

" Come with me. We are closed tomorrow and we can finish tomorrow."

Beth looked at Millie and up the stairs to Millie's room for the night.

Charter 6

1819

P iper was delighted to have real-time with Millie again like they did when they were 5. Christmas was just a day away, and The Little Plantation was a little on the sad side. First Christmas without Sean Jack Little. She was starting to feel pregnant more every day she had done the rabbit test to make sure she was with child, and she was

∞∞∞

Christmas day and she was going to tell her family the good news. Dean came into town to be with his family, and also it was Sara's birthday on the 28th. Dean wants to take Sara with him to the city.

Christmas dinner was small just the family this year, and Tyler's father's Tom was in town also. Just before dessert, getting up from her chair.

"I have some news for all of you here. Tyler and I are going to have a baby." One by one they got up and hugged Piper and Tyler.

∞∞∞

December 28, Sara 17 birthday. Dean asked Sara if she likes to come live with him in the city, till springtime. Sara was all for it, but she asked her mother if it was okay with her. Kitty knew it was a good move for her Sara. Sara could find a nice city man, with her brother.

So sad to see her little sister go. Sara was like Dean, not big on plantation life. Piper asked Sara to write to her every week. The sisters hugged.

She walked into her and Tyler's room and started to cry. He entered the room and saw her crying. He walked over to her and hugged her and kissed her forehead.

"Piper my love you still have me, and Heather and her mother, and Stephen."

"I know, but Sara" she cried harder than before. He put her in the bed and kissed her. She sleeps before he left the room. He looked at his beautiful pregnant wife sleeping.

January 2000

It was a new year and a new time in Millie's life. The Old Little Plantation had been closed for the last two weeks for the holiday. It was January 3, 2000, unlocking the old little plantation for the day, people were waiting for the first tour of the day. Millie is happy to be back at work, telling people all about the Little Plantation and the family who lived here. Every month was different. Millie tells them about the Little family.

Month January and the was 1820. Millie was the only one who did this on the tours. Everyone else just did the outline for the tours. This way she always had the big groups, and up to more than 10 tours a day. Today she had up to 20 tours.

Beth helps Millie on some of her tours today. Loving that Beth was helping her out today. It was the end of the day, and both were very tired. Going up to the room Millie stayed in for the holiday dance to take a nap. Walking up the stairs to the room. Young boy came running down the stairs at her.

"Jack Little Walliams you get back here." Millie looked up to see Piper, but she Piper didn't see her. Millie

" Piper" Still Piper didn't see her, but Jack saw her and said to his mother

"Mommy it is Millie." Piper looked around
" I don't see her Jack."

Jack went up the stairs to Millie as he did that Millie was back in her time at the end of the stairs on the floor.

"Millie are you ok?" Beth looked down at Millie.

"I am not sure." as she got off the floor.

Millie was fine, didn't know why Piper didn't see her. Beth helps her up the stairs to the room again. She got in the bed and Beth went back upstairs to finish closing for the day. In the bed, the room changed on her, and Jack came into the room, he was around 8 years old. He looked at Millie and got in the bed with her

"There you are Miss Millie"

Millie sat up and looked at Jack. Piper came in the room

"Millie"

Piper walked over to her son and Millie. Piper sat on the bed and looked at Millie

" You are still 19?"

" Yes I am and you are not."

Millie was right Piper was 28 now.

Millie and Piper talk for hours as Jack went to get his little sister, so she could meet Millie. Jack came in with his little sister.

"Millie this is my Marie."

Marie was around 5 years old. Millie was waiting for the change again but didn't change back to her time yet. This was the longest time Millie had stayed in Piper time. Millie curious why this was happening now. Piper looked at Millie.

" You look older now what is happening to you."

"What are you talking about?" Millie got up

from the bed and looked in the mirror in the room, and saw that she looked like 28, not 19. Millie turned around looked at Piper, but Piper was gone and the kids also. Millie looked at the mirror again and saw her 19-year-old self again. Millie went down the stairs and saw Beth.

Chapter 7

Piper 1820

Piper was still sad about Sara moving away. She was starting to get the nursery ready for the baby. Tyler was working on business for his father and Plantation. He planned on taking her on his trip for his father, but since Piper expecting a child, and he didn't want something to happen to her or the baby. She was fine with missing the trip this time, but the next one she would be on. She looked forward to Sara's letter every week.

Tyler had been gone on his trip for 2 weeks now, she desperately longed for him. Piper got 7 letters a week from Tyler writing to his Sweetheart. This was the longest she had gone without seeing him since her birthday party. Forgotten who she was in that time before being a wife and soon to be mother. Her mother, Heather, and herself went into town to pick up stuff for the nursery. Heather's birthday was on February 2 and she was going to be 16. Piper wants something nice for her little sister. Heather was not a big party for herself like Piper was, but Heather knew that her sister was missing Father, Sara, and Tyler. So Heather was for the big party this time.

Started planning Heather's birthday party. Kitty help with the planning also, Heather was Kitty's baby, and she wants the world to know who she was in society. Kitty party like this for all her girls at 16.

∞∞∞

Piper was working on paperwork for the plantation one afternoon when the room changed on Piper, and she saw Millie walking around the Plantation with a lot of people. Millie didn't see Piper, so she began to walk with the group. Millie talked about her family in the time that Piper was living in now. Millie talked about the young Heather party, being a sad event in the Little family life again. Piper wants to know why Heather's party would be a sad event, just as the words about to come out Piper were back in her time.

Piper didn't know what to do. Why would Heather's party be a sad event for us? Kitty came in the room and saw Piper crying.

"What is it, my girl?"

"I am fine mother" she was not fine, she wants to tell her mother about Millie.

∞ ∞ ∞

It was a week before Heather's birthday party, and Heather wanted Dean and Sara to come. Piper has sent out the letters to both of them, and that was 2 weeks ago.

A letter came from Tyler saying he was going to be home for Heather's birthday, and that he missed her very much. There was still no word from Dean or Sara. Piper was starting to think this was the sad news she heard in Millie's time, about Heather birthdays being a sad event in the family.

The day before Heather's birthday they got a letter from Dean and in the letter:

"Dear Family, I have some news for you about Sara. Are dear Sara passed away last night from a sickness that does not have a name yet. I was with her at the end. I didn't know she was sick. I was on a trip for work. My family I am coming home with are sweet Sara soon. Love Dean."

Piper looks at the letter Tyler came in the door to see her on the floor crying, with the letter in her hands. Kitty and Heather came into the room, as he read the letter to them.

Millie 2000

Millie tours were so popular that sometimes people would dress in the 1820 wardrobe. Though she saw Piper one day in her tour group, on the day she was talking about Sara's death.

Millie was starting to think there was more to her finding, "Time Pocket" as she called them in her own notebook. Still looking for existing notebooks Piper wrote in every time they met in her time. Asking Beth again if she knew were the notebooks. Beth told that she had them in Piper's old room.

Millie went up to Piper's old room. Walked into the room things changed again. Millie saw crying Piper in her bed.

"Piper" Piper looked up to see Millie.

"Oh, Millie she is gone, my little Sara."

Millie went to her friend from another time and hugged her.

" Piper knows what killed her was scarlet fever."

"Do you know if my Brother Dean was really there for her at the end like his letter said."

" I know what you know about him being there or not. Just what he put in that letter to you guys."

Piper still wants to know why he left her, and didn't tell them about her being sick. Millie saw the notebook on her side table, and the room changed back to her time.

Millie looked around and saw a big teal leather trunk that said Piper notebooks. Opened it up to see 80 notebooks. Picked up the first one and the year was 1810 to the last one saying 1880. There were more than just notebooks in this trunk.

There was a letter to Millie from Piper.

The letter:

"Dear Millie I know you are going to find my notebooks after seeing me tonight, after the death of my Sara. Losing Sara was one of the hardest things in my life, but having Jack and Marie and one other baby. Tyler is always at my side and you are a big part of my life too. I still don't know how the Time Pocket works for us but it does. I love you Millie and soon we will see each other again. Love Always your friend in time Piper May Little-Williams."

Running down the stairs and Beth to help her with trunk and move it to her office. They started to move the trunk the room changed again, but this time they didn't see Piper or Tyler, young man that looked a lot like Tyler, but his eyes.

"What are you doing with my mother's trunk?" Millie looked up at him

"Jack Little is that you?" Jack looked at them

"Yes I am Jack, what are you doing with my mother trunk it is not to leave her room, and I know who you are Millie."

Jack looked mad at her. Both stopped what they were doing. Jack takes his mother trunk back to her room, without looking at them. As he walked out of Piper's room, he was gone again.

I walked back in the room, but now the trunk

had a lock on it. Looking for the key in the room, and didn't find it. Millie went to her office and looked for the key in there, and still nothing. Beth was down at the front desk and there was the key with a note to both of them. Beth went up the stairs to Piper's room where Millie was.

The Note:

"Millie and Beth I am so sorry about Jack sometimes he is a lot like his Grandfather. Here is the key to my trunk, and please keep the trunk in my room. Love Piper."

Opened the trunk again, but one of the notebooks was missing. Notebook that was missing was from the year 1835.

" What happened in 1835?"

"There is not much on record for that year for the Little Plantation."

Millie picked up 10 of the notebooks, from the first one in 1810 to 1820 to her office. She was happy that nothing changed this time.

Chapter 8

Piper 1820

It was two months after Sara's death. Piper was starting to show, and Tyler's birthday April 17. He knew that she had forgotten his birthday, with everything that had happened to lose her father and her sister.

Week before Tyler's birthday, Piper was working on paperwork for the little plantation. Tyler got a letter from his father.

In the letter, Tom was asking his son to help him with shipping, for a month. Tyler didn't know what to do about this, he didn't want to leave his love for a month. Piper was too pregnant to go with him.

Piper was in the sitting room reading a book, walked into the room, and she looked up at him.

"Piper I got a letter from my father, and he needs my help again, and I will be gone for a month."

"Go and help him. I will be fine. I have mother

here, and others, and Dean is coming into town in two weeks."

"Are you sure my love?"

"Yes, we have time before the baby is here. As you can get shipping done for the plantation at the same time. "

He didn't think about that.

"Tyler when are you leaving?"

"On 17."

"Oh on your birthday. We will do something for your birthday the day before."

"You remember." She looked at him and smiled and got up from her chair and walked on him and kissed him.

"I love you Tyler and I will always remember your birthday."

They walked up the stairs to their room.

∞∞∞

The next day Piper was starting to feel like herself again. Started planning something nice and big for Tyler's birthday. Kitty wanted to help Piper with the plantation so she could work on the wife's life. Kitty didn't want Tyler to find another woman in other towns. Kitty never told her girls that their father had two other women. Piper did know about one of her father's ladies.

"Mom I know about dad's other woman,"

"How did you know that?"

"I met her at 14 on the trip I went on with father." Kitty hugged her

" I am so sorry I never told you about them."

"There was more than one woman?"

"Yes, and you have two half-sisters out there."

"Do you know who they are mother?"

"Yes, I do. One of your half-sisters in town and she is 17 almost 18 now, and her name is Lizzie Smith."

"Does she know about us?"

"No, not at all. Lizzie's mother and didn't want her to know who her father is because Sam Smith is."

Piper didn't know what to do with the information that her mother just came to her.

∞∞∞

Day before Tyler's birthday, Piper went all out for his birthday and going away party. Taking Tyler out for the day, like he did for her on their first date. Stephen helped Piper get everything ready. Stephen pulled up in the horse carriage in front of the little plantation. Piper wearing the same cotton green dress the day Tyler took her out 9 months ago. Tyler looked at his beautiful pregnant wife and helped her in the carriage. Stephen took them both to the same spot, but this time the picnic was all set up as they got there.

Tyler helped his lady out again, and Piper walked over to the river and put her feet in the water. Tyler walked over to her and put his arms around her and kissed her neck. She smiled and kissed his hand.

"Piper I can't wait to meet our little one. I wish your father and Sara were here also." She started to tear up at Tyler's words.

"Tyler lets just be us right now. I miss them both so much, but today is a happy day. First time in months, that we are not working on the plantation or you on your ship."

Tyler walked around her and kissed her with so much love in his heart. She kissed him back more with love than she had ever known.

Stephen left the two alone. They sat down on the ground and had their lunch together.

"Thank you, Piper, for a great day out." she looked out to the water.

"Not over yet." one of his smaller boats showed up.

"Tyler will you take me for a ride on one of your boats?" couldn't contain his joy.

"I would love to love, but you are not in boat attire."

Going to the carriage and got some pants and put them on under her skirt, then pulled her skirt down and put it in the carriage. Jasper Wood, one of Tyler's shipmates got out of the boat. Tyler got on the boat Stephen, and Jasper helped Piper in the boat.

In the boat: It was a short ride back to the Little Plantation. She loves being on the boat with him. Tyler came more alive. He had his boat and his girl together. As they got closer to the plantation he stopped the boat and put the anchor down. Tyler got so close to her and held her in his arms.

"Best birthday so far. Thank you Piper, and wish you were coming with me on this trip."

"I do too." She kissed him again.

"I will write to you every day."

"Just come home to me." he looked down at her and smiled.

"I will my love."

2000 Millie

Millie still weirded out by what had happened to her last time the Time Pocket happened. Everyday Millie read up on Piper's notebooks and she was up to the year 1820. Piper wrote to see her 20 times that year, but she never gave the date when they saw each other just a month ago. Millie knew why she did this because 40-year-old Millie told 12-year-old Piper not too.

In the month of April, Millie and the other staff at the old little plantation had school groups come in all month long. Millie likes doing the school groups more than the tour group. Millie works with all the schools in New Orleans. One of the schools wants to do an event at the old little plantation for April 17. Millie and Beth worked with the high school for their reenactor event at the Old Little Plantation.

Twenty high school students sign up for a reenactor event as the old little plantation internship. First internship weekend Millie and Beth worked with 10 students and the other 10 students worked with other staff members. Each group had 5 boys and 5 girls. Millie and Beth let their group know the history of the little plantation and the family that lived here.

Millie was showing the ballroom, where most of the event would take plans. Millie and Beth group recreating Piper coming out party. Millie was unsure about this, but it was going to bring in more money for the upkeep of the Old Little Plantation, and the owner of the little plantation was all about the money. The other group recreating Piper and Tyler's wedding. After all, the students had left Millie and Beth didn't like the whole event, but their hands were tied.

After a month of helping their group, it was the day of the event. The event was bigger than Millie and Beth thought it would be. Millie went up the stairs in Piper's old room and sat on the bed. The room changed to Millie and she saw Piper looking out the window.

"Piper."

Piper sees a 19-year-old Millie. Piper was in her 50's.

"So young my Millie."

Millie got up from the bed and walked to Piper. Millie knew it was 1850 by her closes. Piper had been crying.

"What is going on Piper, why so sad?"

"My Tyler and Jack are lost at sea." Millie hugged her friend

"Do you want to tell them what happened to them?" Piper pulled away

"Yes."

"They will be home tomorrow. The date is April 17 1850 right?" Piper knotted at Millie.

"Is this my notebooks?"

"No, it is in little plantation history books. Tyler wrote them in your family story-book, each generation to read and know all about you and Tyler's love story."

The look on Piper's face said it all, didn't know he was doing that.

"Went did he start the book?"
Millie laughed

"The day after your coming out party." Piper hugged Millie

"Thank you so much."

Millie let go of Piper and she was gone again.

Millie in the room again alone, she was glad

to give Piper good news. Millie sometimes wants to stay in Piper time, but at the same time being 20-century girl life was a little better, and being into girls, would not have worked in Piper time. Millie would have to marry a man before 20 and that was not for her at all. Beth came into the room.

"There you are. You are going to miss it." Millie did want to see her and Beth group do their thing.

Millie got to the ballroom just to see Piper look alike and Tyler look-alike recreating from Tyler journals about his and Piper's first dance. The owner of the little plantation came next to Millie and Beth

"Wow look at that just like the way my grandma Little told me."

Millie and Beth looked at the 35-year-old man.

"You are part of the Little tree?"

"Yes, I am. Piper is my 2nd great grand-mother. You guys didn't know. That ok you know now, and the name is Ben Little."

"You two are the best. The holiday event was the best the little plantation had since Piper lived here. I need to get the money from the event."

Ben walked away from them and both looked at each other

"he looks identical his 2nd great grand-father Tyler"

Chapter 9

Piper 1820

Tyler had been gone for two weeks, and Piper really started working in a baby room. Piper looked into both her half-sisters. Piper went into town to get to know Lizzie. Piper knows Charlotte to be one of Lizzie's friends in town. Piper had it all planned out, how she was going to meet Lizzie. Stephen took her into town. Lizzie worked at a fabric store, and Piper couldn't wait to talk to Lizzie.

As Piper walked into the fabric store she saw a girl that looked so much like her Sara. Piper started to cry, Lizzie walked over to Piper.

"Are you okay Miss?"

Piper had no words. Lizzie didn't know what to do about this crying very pregnant woman.

"I am sorry you look so much like my sister that passed away back in February" Lizzie just hugged her

"You are Sara Little sister. I was friends with

her." Piper looked at Lizzie and smiled.

"Sara was the best sister in the world. How did you and Sara meet?"

"At school, before she moved to the city."

Lizzie started to cry. Lizzie and Piper cried and hugged. After all that Piper asked Lizzie to come to the plantation for lunch next week, and Lizzie said yes.

Piper got home after a trip into town. Piper was so happy to meet Lizzie. Piper went up the stairs to the baby room. Piper sat in the rocking chair that Stephen had made for her. Piper looked down at her growing belly and put her hand on her belly.

"Piper I am home."

Piper looked up and saw Tyler in the doorway looking at Piper with a smile. Piper got up and ran to Tyler and hugged and kissed him. Piper and Tyler walked back to their room.

The next day Piper was overjoyed that Tyler was home two weeks easily. Tyler's father Tom didn't need him as long as he thought. Piper told Tyler all about meeting Lizzie and how she looked a lot like Sara, and that she was coming over for lunch next week. Tyler asked if she told her mother about this. Piper didn't tell her mother because her mother and Heather were on a trip to the city to see Dean.

One week later: Piper went all out for

her lunch with Lizzie. Lizzie showed up and Tyler met her at the front door and took her to the dining room. Lizzie had never been in The Little Plantation, because of her mother not letting her. The Little Plantation was everything the plantation was. Tyler pulled out Lizzie's chair and Lizzie sat down. Piper came into the room and Tyler pulled out her chair for her also. Tyler sat next to Piper. Lunch was everything both Piper and Lizzie wanted. After lunch, Piper took Lizzie around the whole Little Plantation and told her stories about her father. Lizzie was not sure why Piper was telling her all about her family as if Lizzie was her family. Lizzie was the only child of her mother and her father Sam Smith. As Lizzie was about to leave Piper handed her a note, and said read after you get home.

2000 Millie

Millie had a day off from doing tours. Millie was working on a summer event for the Old Little Plantation. The owner Ben wanted to do more events at the little plantation, like his parents did in the 1980s. Millie liked the idea and Beth helped Millie plan the summer event. It was the start of May, and the summer event would be in June and July, and a special anniversary event on August 3.

Millie and Beth were staying at the old little plantation for the 4 months to get all the planning done for the summer events every month. Ben likes that Beth and Millie both stay at the plantation. Ben wants to open the little plantation up as an Inn. Ben wanted both Millie and Beth to live at the plantation. Millie moved back into the old little plantation and rented out her place why she lived in the plantation. Millie moved into Piper's old room.

Beth started hiring more people for the Old Little Plantation. The changes at the Plantation were starting to show. Millie came down the stairs to find Piper in the sitting room. Millie went over to her and then she was gone. Beth came into the room after Millie.

"Millie are you ok?"

"Yes, why?"

"Millie you looked like a woman in her 50 walking into this room, but now you are 19 again."

Millie didn't know what to say to Beth.

That night after everyone had gone Millie was the only one in the Plantation, Beth was working out moving into the plantation. Millie was waiting for the first guest to stay at the Old Little Plantation Inn. Millie was in the sitting room reading a book. Millie heard the bell from the front desk. Millie got up and walked to the front desk and no one was there. The room changed on Millie and she saw Piper walking down the stairs

"Millie you are here."

Piper was 19 and very pregnant. Millie walked up the stairs to her and hugged her. Both Piper and Millie walked down the stairs to the sitting room.

"Hello Miss"

Millie was back in her time looking at the family that was going to stay at the old little plantation Inn.

"Hello Welcome To The Old Little Plantation Inn. I am Millie."

Millie goes there by reservation. Millie showed them their rooms for the next 4 days.

Millie closed up the big doors for the night and went back to the sitting room. Piper was in the sitting room waiting for her. Millie tells Piper all about how her 2nd grandson was making the plantation into an Inn. Piper like what was happening with her family home. One of the kids came into the sitting room, and Piper was gone again.

One of the kids asked if there was some food. Millie walked them to the kitchen and asked made them what they would like. Both just wanted a PB&J. Millie them two PB&J. Both kids said thank you and went back to their room. Millie cleaned up and walked back to the sitting room, and back to her book. It was around 9:30 pm and Millie walked up the stairs and checked on the family to see if they needed something before she went to bed, and they didn't. Millie walked to her room and went to bed for the night.

Chapter 10

1820 Piper

Summertime at the little Plantation. Piper and Tyler are getting things ready for their little one. Piper mostly stayed in the house. Kitty Rose and Heather had decided to move to the city with Dean. Piper knew why they wanted to stay because Heather had met a young man on the trip. Piper was happy for her little sister.

Piper was in the sitting room quilting a blanket for her little one. Tyler was out for the day in town, and he asked the staff to keep an eye on Piper. Stephen was always up to keep Piper company. Stephen was in his late 30s and had been with the Little his whole life. The Little family was good to their staff at the plantation. Piper went up the stairs to take a nap.

Piper was in her room and saw that her room changed and she saw no one. Piper walked around the room and saw the calendar on the wall and it said the year 2000 and the month it was on was June. Piper started walking to the door and the room changed back. Piper went back to her bed and had a nap.

Tyler came home and asked Stephen where Piper was and he told upstairs taking a nap. Tyler went to the baby room and put a little toy down in the bassinet. Tyler couldn't wait to meet his little one. Tyler walked out of the room to see Piper coming out of their room.

"Did you have a nice nap Piper?" Piper smiled at Tyler and knotted.

They both walked down the stairs to have dinner.

The next day Piper wants to go into town to see Lizzie. Tyler went with her. Tyler dropped Piper off at the fabric store because the other business to take care of for the plantation. Piper walked into the fabric store, but Piper didn't see Lizzie in them. Piper asked the other girl where Lizzie was. The other didn't know. Piper walked out of the fabric store and went to the cafe across the street and sat at one of the tables outside. Piper sat there drinking tea and little sandwiches. Piper looked down at her belly and saw the baby inside her.

" Can you sit here with you?" Piper knew that voice anywhere it was her Tyler.

"Yes, you may."

Tyler sat next to her. She told him that Lizzie

was not at the bookstore today.   "Let's get you home." Tyler helps Piper up and in the carriage.

2000 Millie

Millie had been working and living at the Plantation for 2 weeks before Beth moved into the Plantation. The Little Plantation Inn was a very popular New Orleans. Millie was still doing tours at the plantation. Millie was in her office working on the June event at the end of the month. Beth is waiting for a new guest downstairs. Millie made up some flyers on the computer for the summer event. There was a knock on the door.

"Come on in" Beth walked in.

"Millie that the last guest had shown up."

Going downstairs with Beth and having dinner. Millie gave Beth a big smile, and got up and walked to Beth and gave her a kiss.

"I would love Beth." Beth kissed Millie back, and they walked down the stairs to the dining room.

Beth had ordered them some pizza which was Millie's favorite. Millie sat down and got 2 slices of pizza. Millie and Beth talked about work and their relationship. June 25th was Beth's birthday and that was the date for the first summer event.

Millie and Beth cleaned up. Millie closed the big doors for the night. Beth went to make sure all the guests were good for the night. Millie walked up behind Beth and put her arms around her and kissed her neck.

"Come to me to my room I have something for you."

Millie opened her door and Beth walked in. Beth sat on the bed. Millie pulled out something from the closet.

" I know it is 2 weeks before your birthday, but I couldn't wait to give this to you." Millie was holding a small box, and she gave it to Beth.

Beth opened it to see a pair of pearl earrings. Beth face light up at her present and kissed Millie.

"I love them, and thank you."

The June summer event was great for The Little Plantation Inn. Millie was up to 30 hours a day. At night was the only time Millie and Beth had to be together. Millie wanted to tell Beth about seeing Piper every night until she moved into the plantation. Life at the old little plantation had changed for Millie and Beth. June was over before they knew it. Working on the July event was very special for the owner Ben. This July 30 event was in honor of this Great Grand-Father Jack Little Williams's birthday. Millie and Beth work hard on this event. Ben wanted to be part of the planning of this event.

Chapter 11

1820 Piper

July was here and one month before Piper and Tyler's child would be born. Piper was working on the finishing touch in the nursery. Piper's mother Kitty was back at the plantation to help Piper. Heather stayed in the city with her new suitor. Piper was sad that Heather didn't come with their mother, but Piper knew Heather was in good hands. Tyler was working on business for his father and the plantation.

Piper stayed up in the nursery most days, but at night she sat in the sitting room. Most every night Piper saw Millie her friend from another time. Piper glad on the night she and Millie could meet and talk. The last night Piper saw Millie in the sitting room was almost 3 weeks now. Piper did tell Tyler all about seeing Millie almost every night.

Kitty made sure there was a midwife to help with the delivery of her first grandchild. Life at the plantation was a little crazy, waiting for Piper to give birth. Piper was quite big and she was ready to give birth, and have her body back and to meet her little one. Piper was hoping that it would be a boy. Millie told her that she would have two children, but she never told her what she was having. On July 29 Kitty went into town to pick up supplies. Kitty went past the bookstore, and Lizzie came out and stopped Kitty. Lizzie asked how Piper was doing, Kitty was unsure why Lizzie wanted to know. Lizzie gave Kitty a little toy to give to Piper.

Kitty got home and Stephan helped bring in the supplies. Kitty went upstairs to find Piper in her bed.

"Mommy it is time" Kitty called out for the midwife to Piper's room.

Tyler was right there with the midwife. Tyler sat next to Piper and kissed her forehead.

"Tyler you don't have to be here."

"I am not leaving her side." Kitty let Tyler stay.

The Birth: Tyler was right by Piper's side the whole time. This was new to the midwife and Kitty, but he wants to be part of this moment. Piper delivery was normal. Piper gave birth to a boy, and everything with him was good. Kitty cleaned him and wrapped him in the quilt Piper made for him. Kitty walked him over to Piper and Tyler. Piper opened her arms and her mother put him in her arms. Tyler kissed Piper's forehead and looked down at his son and kissed him.

"Piper, what do you want to call him?" Piper looked at Tyler and back at her little boy in her arms.

"Jack Little Williams." Kitty Rose started to cry.

Tyler kissed her. Jack Little Williams's birthday July 30 1820 at 2 am.

2000 Millie

Millie was sleeping in her bed at The Little Plantation Inn, she woke to a baby crying in the room next to her. Millie got up and walked to the side door to her room. Millie went into the room and saw Piper in a rocking chair with baby Jack in her arms. Millie walked over to them.

"Oh Piper he is so handsome."

Piper looked up and saw Millie and smiled and cried at the same time.

Millie saw that the sun was rising and the room changed back into the storage room for the books. Millie went back to her room and saw Beth waiting for her in the room. Beth told Millie about hearing baby Jack cry also. Millie and Beth got back into the bed, and went back asleep.

Around 8 am Millie got up and looked at Beth sleeping next to her. Millie likes the idea of waking up next to Beth every day. Beth opened her eyes with a smile.

"I saw that." Millie kissed her, and Beth pulled her back in bed.

They laid there for some time. Millie looked over at the clock on the wall, and it said 8:30. Millie got up and so did Beth. Beth did have some of her clothes in Millie's room, just for a day like today. Both were in 1820 clothes.

Beth was in the storage room to go down the stairs and Millie went out her door. Millie saw Ben at the front door in 1820 clothes. Millie almost called him Tyler, because he looked so much like his 2nd great grandfather. They all had two hours before people going to be showing up for the event. The guest at the Inn started coming down, and the dining room all set up for breakfast.

Millie was outside in the courtyard set up storytelling of The Little Plantation. Millie and Beth going to do the storytelling tonight. Beth came over to Millie and started helping. The other staff was worker other spots. They were all doing the finishing touch for the day event.

Millie went back in the house after she was done. As Millie walked up to the front door she saw a young girl in real 1820 clothes sitting on the porch chair. Millie walked over to her.

"Who are you?" Lizzie looked up.

"I am Lizzie Smith and I am friends with the lady of the house Piper."

Millie waited to see if time would change

back, and it didn't.

"Miss Lizzie I will go get her for you."

Millie walked into the house, and she was still in 1820. Tyler was coming down the stairs and saw Millie.

Chapter 12

1820 Piper

Tyler went down the stairs to Millie.

"Millie you are here, Piper will be so happy, come with me and met our son Jack."

"Tyler there is a girl named Lizzie outside wanting to see Piper and baby Jack."

"I know I will get her soon." Tyler walked Millie up the stairs to the nursery. Millie open the door and saw Piper in the rocking chair with baby Jack in her arms. Piper looked and smile at Millie. Millie sat next to Piper.

"Would you like to hold him?"

"I would love to."

Piper handed Jack to Millie, this was not Millie's first time holding a baby.

Tyler came in with Lizzie right next to him. Piper got up and huge Lizzie. Tyler walked over to Millie and she gave him baby Jack. Piper was done hugging Lizzie and saw the Millie was gone. Piper walked on Tyler with their little boy in his arms. Piper took baby Jack from Tyler, and it was time to feed the little one. Tyler walked Lizzie out.

Tyler saw Millie again with another man. Millie walked over to Tyler and she was gone, but the other man was not. Tyler walked over to him and the room changed on him. Millie turned around and saw Tyler in her time, and next to his 2nd great-grandson.

"Millie?"

Millie grabbed Tyler's hand and took him in the other room.

"Tyler you are in my time and year is 2000. This is an event to honor Jack birthday. The man you standing next in your 2nd great-grandson."

Tyler looked at her not knowing what to say.

Millie and Tyler went looking for Beth and hoped that Tyler would go back to his time, but Millie didn't how they were the Time Pocket were at in the house. Looking for Beth for 20 mins they find her.

"How is he here."

"I don't know."

Millie told Beth to start the event outside and she was going to take Tyler to the room and see if the Time Pocket was working up there.

As Millie and Tyler walked into the room they were both back in 1820. Piper came out of the nursery to see Millie and Tyler in their room. Piper walked over to Tyler and hugged him.

"Tyler you have been gone for 4 hours." Millie looked at Piper

"Are you sure?"

" Yes I am I feed baby Jack every 4 hours and I was feeding him before Tyler was gone and I just fed him again."

Millie needs to get back to her time but how? Millie left the room and as she did she was back in her time.

∞∞∞

Piper kissed Tyler and they both laid down in their bed still kissing. What a day they both had. Piper closed her eyes and was asleep. Tyler got up from the trying not wake up Piper. Tyler walked into the nursery and saw his sleeping son in his bassinet. Tyler was happy to know that his line would be still going strong in the year 2000, he just wished he knew his name.

2000 Millie

It was the day after the July summer event. what day it was for Millie. Beth and Millie both got the next two days off doing tours for the little plantation, just working at night work for the Inn. Millie was in her room and Beth had stayed the night in Millie's room. Millie did have the bigger room. Millie didn't want to leave the room, Beth wanted to go to a movie and lunch just the two of them. Millie and Beth went to see the X Men movie, and lunch in the French Quarter area for lunch.

It has been some time since Millie and Beth had a real date that was out of the little plantation walls. Millie and Beth talked and laughed they walked hand and hand down the street. They got to the movie theater and got their tickets and walked into the theater room and sat in the back row.

Millie and Beth got back to the little plantation with time to be alone in Millie's room, before doing the night check. The day out was just what they needed in their relationship they had been together for 9 months now, and it was time to take that next step in their relationship. Millie went to her room door with Beth, Millie grabbed Beth by the waist and took her into the room and started kissing her. Beth grabbed Millie's ass and kissed her back. They made love for the first time.

Millie got up around 8 am the next day and went down to get some food for her and Beth. Beth still sleeping. Millie walked down the stairs to the kitchen to find Ben there. Ben looked at Millie.

" Having a nice day off I see." with a cute smile on his face.

"Best days off ever."

Ben smiled again

"Who was that guy walking around with you the day of the event?"

Millie didn't know what to say to him.

"He was a guest of the Inn I think."

Ben went with it this time, but he knew that man from somewhere before.

"You and Beth can have the night off tonight. I am going to stay tonight and help the guest. You both do a great job here in my Old family house."

"Have you ever lived here with your family?"

"Yes, I did back in 1985 right before the last event my father put on before he died. The thing that was for Piper Little birthday event." Millie stepped back

"I was at the party when I was only 5, but I remember it very well."

Millie sat next to Ben and they talked about that event, this was the first time in a long time he could come back here to his family home. Everything Millie had done in the year she had been there helped him came back to this place, that he loved as a child.

Millie got up and walked out of the kitchen and back up to the room with Beth. Beth sitting in the bed waiting for Millie. Millie put the food on the table and Beth walked over and kissed Millie.

"Last night was amazing, and we have the night off also."

Millie just kissed her. They both ate the food, and Beth went back to bed. They stayed in bed all day and night.

Chapter 13

1820 Piper

Piper woke up to baby Jack crying and walked to his room, and saw Tyler about to pick up Jack. Tyler had baby Jack in his arms and looked at Piper.

"Happy Birthday my love." and walked over to her and kissed her.

Piper smiled and kissed him back. Piper sat in the rocking chair and Tyler took baby Jack to her and put him in her arms. It was feeding time for baby Jack. Tyler sat next to them watching with love in his eyes, his wife and the mother of his son.

Later that afternoon Kitty Rose came up to baby Jack's room and saw Piper had fallen asleep in the rocking chair. Kitty pick up baby Jack and took him downstairs to the sitting room. Kitty was so in love with her little grandson. Kitty started to cry looking down at him, wished her Jack (Sean Jack Little) was here with her. Piper came into the room and saw her mother and her son. Piper sat next to her mother.

"Happy Birthday my sweet girl"

Tyler wanted to do something nice for Piper today on her birthday. It had been a year now since they had their first dance. Tyler asked Stephen and the other staff to help him set up the ballroom for him and Piper tonight. Kitty was part of the planning as well. Tyler went into the sitting room and saw Kitty, Piper, and baby Jack. Tyler picked up baby Jack and took him back to his room. Piper stayed with her mother in the sitting room.

Tyler put baby Jack in his bed. Tyler watched his son sleep. Piper came into the room and saw Tyler watching their son sleeping. Piper put her arms around Tyler. They both walked back to their room.

∞∞∞

It was dinner time and Kitty Rose put baby Jack down for Piper. Tyler took Piper down the stairs to the ballroom. The staff of the plantation set up the ballroom just like it did a year ago. Piper looked around the ballroom and started to cry. Tyler hugged her and kissed her.

"I know it's not much Piper, but what to thank you for being my wife and mother of our son."

Tyler took Piper's hand and went to the dance floor. Music started to play and they started dancing. Piper was 20 now, and far from the girl, she was a year ago.

Millie 2000

Millie woke up to Beth while holding a lemon cupcake with white frosting.

"Happy birthday Millie and happy one year working here." Millie kissed Beth

"Thank you."

" I am taking you out for dinner tonight after your last tour of the day." Millie smiled and kissed Beth again.

Beth went out the other door. Millie got dressed in her tour wardrobe. Beth was working at the front desk today. Millie first tour showed up. Millie had special plans for her tours today. Millie talked about baby Jack and Piper birthday being so close together.

Millie did 20 tours on her 20th birthday. 20 is Millie's favorite number after all. Beth asked one of their co-workers to watch the front desk tonight why she and Millie went out for Millie's birthday dinner. Millie in her room getting ready for her date with Beth.

The room changed on Millie, walking into the other room, it was not a nursery. Millie walked out in the hall and saw no one. Millie walked down the stairs and went to the sitting room, and still no one. Millie sat in one of the chairs and waited. Millie didn't know what year she was in. Millie got up and walked outside to see if she could see someone.

Millie went back in her room, or Piper she still didn't know. Millie know she was in the 1800's because she had to light a candle in the room. Millie looking around the room to see the clue "Time Pocket" she was in and how to get back to her time. Millie started to cry thinking she was never going to get back to Beth and her life in the year 2000. Millie laid down in bed and fell asleep.

Millie woke up the next morning still not in her time. Millie had a better look at the room looked a lot like Piper's room, but also not. Millie got out of the bed and walked down the stairs and saw a man. Millie walked up to the man and the room changed on her and saw Beth.

Millie ran to Beth crying. Beth hugged Millie so heard and they both walked up to Millie's room. Beth closed the door and looked over at Millie.

"Were you with Piper?"

Millie cried "No. I don't know what year I was in, but there was no one in the house all night."

Beth walked over to Millie and hugged her

again.

Millie sat on her bed with Beth and told her all about what happened to her. Beth went into the storage room and got one the book about the time went the Old Little Plantation had no one living in the house. Millie looked in the book and saw photos of her room in the time she may have been in. It was around 1888 about 8 years after Piper passed away. Millie wanted to know why she keeps finding "Time Pocket" in this plantation.

Chapter 14

1820 Piper

Baby Jack is months old now. Piper's life had changed so much after Jack was born. Kitty Rose Piper's mother was staying for one more month, before going back to the city with Heather and Dean. Piper did want Heather and Dean to come back to the plantation just to meet baby Jack, but Heather was too busy with her young man in the city. Heather was staying with Dean.

Piper wrote Heather and Dean a letter two weeks ago. Dean wrote her back and told her that he and Heather are coming back to the plantation just before their Kitty (their mother) came back to the city. Dean also let her know that Heather's young man was also coming with them to meet her. Piper was happy about the news.

Tyler was working with his father in town on the shipping business. Piper wants to tell her mother about Lizzie and her friends she was start-

ERIN MARIE COURTNEY

ing to have with her half-sister. Had not told Lizzie that they were half-sister. Piper asked Tyler's
shipmate Jasper to look for her other half-sister.

Piper hoping soon she would see Millie soon.
The last time she saw her was on the day Jack was
born. Piper working on paperwork for the plantation as baby Jack was taking a nap.

Tyler and Jasper walked into the house with a
big box for Piper. Tyler left it in the sitting room
and went to go look for his wife. Tyler went to the
nursing no Piper just sleeping, Jack. Tyler went to
his and Piper's room and there she was at the desk
and she fell asleep at the desk. Tyler walked over
to her and kissed her head and he did she woke up
and looked up to him with a smile.

Tyler grabbed her hand and took her down to
the sitting room where he left the big box for her.
Piper's eyes got so big looking at the big box.

"It's for you my love."

Piper walked over to the big box and opened
it and saw a new side table for the sitting room.
Piper walked over to Tyler and kissed him.

"I love it." Piper put the side table next to
her chair. Piper saw that there was more in the box
10 new books. Piper looked up at Tyler and smiled
at him. She pulled out each book one by one.

The list of books in the box Pride and Preju-
dice, Frankenstein, Sense and Sensibility, Emma,
Persuasion, Northanger, The Complete Grimm's
Fairy Tales, Mansfield Park, Ivanhoe, and The
Swiss Family Robinson. Tyler helped Piper put the

books on the bookshelf in the sitting room.

Piper went back to baby Jack's room as was feeding time again. Piper gets back to baby Jack's room and opens the door to find her mother holding Jack.

Piper walked on to her rocking chair and sat down. Kitty walked over to Piper and handed over baby Jack to her.

2000 Millie

It had been two weeks since Millie's birthday and the night she was in 1888. Millie asked Beth to move into her room. Millie didn't want to be alone like that night again. The day time Millie was okay, she loved doing her tours. There was a waiting list for Millie tours now at the Old Little Plantation. Ben Little the owner of the Old Little Plantation wanted to start doing once month night tour by Millie and Beth.

Being with Millie was Beth's happy place. Was the first night for the monthly time tour at The Old Little Plantation Inn. Some of the people for the tour were staying at the Inn also. Millie and Beth waited at the front desk for everyone to show up, there around 20 people on the list.

Millie started her nighttime tour a little different than her day tours. They started off in the ballroom and had everyone sit down in the chair. Millie and Beth in front of all of them. Millie started talking to a group of people as the room changed on her again, Millie tried to grab Beth hand to stay in her time. Millie was all alone in a very dark ballroom.

After the first time this happens, Millie always carried a flashlight and she turned it on to see no one. Millie walked out of the room and up the stairs to her room, and open the door to find Piper sitting on the bed. There was light in the room so Millie put the flashlight away. Millie looked at Piper was an old lady in her 70.

"Well, Millie it is about time you came back here to see me." Piper looked at Millie and saw that she was 20.

"Oh wait you are not the Millie I know." Millie didn't know what to say.

"Millie talk to me."

"Piper what are you talking about coming back to you?"

As Piper was about to tell her the room changed back to Millie again.

Millie walked out of her room and down the stairs to the ballroom and everyone was still there. Millie walked over to Beth.

"How long was I gone?"

"Not long at all. The lights went out right as you disappeared."

"So no one saw me disappear?"

"That's right Millie."

Millie and Beth started the tour.

∞∞∞

After the tour and people started leaving or going back to the rooms at the Inn. Millie sat down in the sitting room, and Beth sat next to her and asked about what happened. Millie told Beth everything. They walked up the stairs to their room. As soon as Millie closed the door she started kissing Beth like she was never going to see her again. Beth kissed back the same way.

Chapter 15

1820 Piper

Piper was waiting for Heather and Dean to show up today. Piper got baby Jack dressed up to meet his aunt and uncle. Tyler moved one of Jack's bassinets in the sitting room. Piper's heart full of love as both Heather and Dean came up the driveway to the house. Tyler was holding baby Jack so Piper could hugged Heather and Dean.

Dean got out of the carriage first to help out woman Piper didn't know. On the other side, a young man got out to help Heather out. Piper ran out to Heather and gane her a great big hug.

"I have missed you so much." Heather started to cry as did Piper.

The young man was around 20.

"I am Wesley Lee Miller."

Piper stopped hugging Heather and looked at Wesley and hugged him.

Dean and thelady came around the carriage to

see Piper hugging Wesley. As soon as Piper saw Dean she stopped hugging Wesley, and ran over to Dean and hugged him. Dean stop the hugged and took Emily's hand.

" Piper. This is Emily Ann Little, my wife."

Piper looked at Dean then at Emily and smiled and hugged Emily.

∞∞∞∞

In the sitting room, Heather was the first to hold the baby Jack. Piper asked Dean and Emily how the met and everything. Dean told Piper and his mother they story of how he met Emily.

Piper took baby Jack back to his room for a nap. Heather came up with Piper. Heather asked Piper what she thinks of Wesley. Piper put baby Jack down and smiled at her little sister.

" I like him, and he really likes you. He looks at you the same way Tyler looked at me. Heather, is he the one for you?"

Heather smiled at her big sister.

"I think so, but I am still too young to think about forever with Wesley."

"Good to know my sister."

Piper walked Heather to her old room.

"I got you something."

Heather opens the door to her room to see Piper's plum-colored dress.

"I know you love this dress, and I want you to

have it now." Heather hugged Piper.

Piper leveled Heather in her room. Piper went down the stairs and saw Emily.

" Emily would like a tour of the plantation?"

"I would love one."

Piper and Emily walked out to the courtyard. Piper and Emily talked like old friends.

"Are you with child?"

Emily smiled and looked down at her belly.

"Yes."

Piper and Emily walked back to the house.

∞∞∞

In baby Jack's room, Piper and Tyler talked about Dean and Emily. Piper was feeding Jack. Tyler talked about Sean Jack Little Will. If Dean did get married he could take the plantation from them. Tyler went to the room and got the Will to read over again, before going down to dinner with it. Piper was done feeding baby Jack, and it was his bedtime.

At dinner:

Kitty Rose looked at the Will first. Kitty knew more about Sean Jack Little's last words for the Will. Kitty told them all their father's last wish was for Piper and Tyler to have The Little Plantation and their children. Dean had no problem letting Piper and Tyler and their children can have the Plantation. They all signed saying that Piper and Tyler and the children own or live in The Little Plantation.

At the end of the night, everyone went to bed, but Piper stayed in the sitting room reading one of her new books. Piper was hoping that she would see Millie tonight. It was a little after midnight and the room changed on Piper and she saw Millie sitting next to her. Millie looked over to see Piper next to her.

"Millie I am happy to see you, my friend."

Millie

Millie was so happy to see Piper and to see they both the same age. It was September 1, 1820. Millie knew she was in Piper time not her. Piper put the book down.

"How did you know I needed you tonight?"

"I was just going to say the same thing to you."

Millie and Piper talked about everything in their life. Piper asked Millie to come up with her to check on Jack. Millie followed Piper to Jack's room. Jack was up and ready for feeding. Millie sat down in the chair and had fallen asleep in baby Jack's room.

Millie woke up the next day still was in baby Jack's room, and saw Piper also asleep in her rocking chair. Millie didn't know what to do and why she was still in Piper's time. Millie got up and went back down the stairs to the sitting room, hoping she could find the "Time Pocket". Millie sat in the same chair she did the night before. As she did Jasper 6'1" blue-gray eyes dark brown long curly in his face with cowboy-like looking at Millie.

"Who are you?"

"This is my friend Millie from town,"
Piper walked into the sitting room.

"Millie is staying with us for a day or two."
Millie red in the face looked at Piper and walked over to Piper.

"Millie let me show you to your room."

Piper showed Millie the room she was going to stay in or something.

"Millie this was my sister Sara's room, and some of her old clothes are still here. I think you should change."

"Thank you. Who was that man?"

" That is Jasper Wood. Tyler's business partner and he is staying in the guest house."

Piper let Millie change. Millie laid down on the bed feel intrigued by this cowboy-like man she just met in 1820.

With Beth in 2000:

Beth wakes up the next day to see that Millie was not in bed. Beth knew Millie liked going down to the sitting room at night in the hope she will see Piper. In the sitting room no Millie. Beth looked all over the plantation still no Millie. Beth went back to their room and hoped Millie would be back. Still no Millie so Beth went to Piper's old trunk and looked in Piper notebooks to see if there was something about Millie on September 1, 1820, and other years. Beth saw a note with her name on it and in Millie's handwriting.

The note:

"Dear Beth, I am in 1820 with Piper and I am staying in Sara Little's old room. I am hoping no one is in that room. The room number should be 20 in our time. I am not sure how to get back, but I will leave more notes in Sara's room (20). I have been here for almost a week now. I love you Beth and hopefully soon I will get back to you soon. Love Millie."

Beth put the note on the side table. Beth went back down to the front desk to see who was in room 20. No one, but the last person who stayed in room 20 was Ben Little.

Chapter 16

1820

Piper loved having Millie staying in Sara's old room. Millie had been there for almost two weeks. Dean, Emily, Heather, Wesley, and Kitty (Piper's mother) had all gone back to the city two weeks now.

Piper knew Millie wanted to get back to her time, but Piper didn't want her to go yet. Millie stayed in Sara's old room for two weeks. Tyler told Piper you should let Millie go back home. Piper knew he was right, but Piper didn't know why Millie was staying for so long this time.

Millie missed Beth so much, and she didn't know what to do in this time. Millie helped Piper with baby Jack and did go into the town two times last week. Millie missed her time and tried everything she could find the time pocket in the plantation.

Millie wrote notes to Beth and hoped they got to her. Sara's old room was where Millie wanted to feel close to Beth. Millie writing in a notebook about her time in 1820. She did this to help her with her tours once she is back in her time.

Tyler and Piper wanted to take baby Jack for his first boat ride. They did ask Millie if she wanted to come with them. Millie said no, it was because she wanted to have the plantation to herself so she could go and be in Piper and Tyler's room in the hope that she could find a time pocket. Millie walked in the room and nothing happened.

Out on the boat, Piper and Tyler and baby Jack were having family time. Baby Jack was two months old now. Tyler enjoying having his family to himself. He liked Millie.

"Piper my love. I know you want Millie to stay, but I hope she is gone when we get back. I miss you and our time together."

Piper looked at Tyler.

" I miss you too. I do hope she finds a way back home."

Tyler kissed Piper and baby Jack grabbed his daddy hair. Tyler grabbed Jack from Piper and took him in front of the boat wheel and baby Jack started laughing. Piper smiled at the sight of her two boys happy.

Piper and Tyler got back just before sunset. Tyler took baby Jack to his bed. Piper went to Sara's old room to see if Millie was still there. She opened the door and saw no one. She walked back to her and Tyler's room and saw Tyler in their bed.

"Come to me, Piper." Piper walked over to the bed.

"Millie is gone. I think she is back in her time." Tyler grabbed Piper and pulled her in the bed with him.

"I know" Tyler and Piper started kissing.

2000

Millie wakes up in her own bed.

"BETH." Beth came out of the storage room next to there room.

"MILLIE you are back." Millie got off the bed to Beth and kissed her. Millie and Beth into the bed and made love like there was no tomorrow.

Millie had been in 1820 for over a month. It was now Oct. 9, 2000. Beth looked at Millie.

"I have missed you so much."

Millie just kissed Beth. Millie and Beth stayed in their room the whole day.

∞∞∞

The next day Millie went down the stairs to start her day. Millie was looking forward to doing her tours. Beth had told Ben that Millie had a family emergency and that why she was gone for a month. Millie walked up to the front desk to look list name for her tours today. Millie was happy to see she had 21 tours down on the list.

The first group show up for Millie's tour of the day. Beth was at the front desk smiling at Millie. Millie walked her tour group to the ballroom.

"Welcome Everyone To The Old Little Plantation. The Plantation build 1700 by Robert Benjamin Little. I will be walking all you into the past. Robert's grandson Sean Jack Little, took over the Plantation after his father passed away when he was 21 years old. In 1795 Sean Jack Little was married, Kitty Rose Moore. They had their son Dean Little in 1796. Piper May Little was born August 3, 1800." Millie walked her group around the whole Plantation talking about the Little family.

Millie told more about Piper and Tyler's life at the Plantation. Millie did have more to tell her tour groups, because of her month in Piper time. At the end of every tour group, she let them know that next month will have a new story to tell them about the Piper and Tyler.

The last tour group left for the day. Millie back to her room with Beth at her side. Millie and

Beth did the Inn part of the job, they could be in their wardrobe. Millie had the front desk tonight checking in the guest for the Inn. Beth checked on the rooms for the guest coming in to stay. Beth went in room 20 and saw Piper on the bed. Piper was in her 20. Beth walked over to her.

"You are Beth right?"

" I am her."

"Millie is back in your time right?" Beth smiled at Piper.

" Yes two days ago." Piper hugged Beth, and after Piper hugged Beth she was gone.

Beth was done with the rooms check walked down the stairs to the front desk and saw Millie checking in a family that was staying at the Inn. Beth took over the front, and Millie walked the family up to their rooms for the week. Millie came back down to the front with Beth. Millie had Beth hand under the desk so no one could see them holding hands.

"Beth I can't wait to get back in my bed tonight." Beth blushed at Millie words.

"I have to tell you I saw Piper in room 20. Piper was happy to know you are home and safe."

Millie didn't care if someone saw her kiss, Beth.

"Just 20 more minutes to go."

It was now 9 pm and The Old Little Plantation was closed for the night. Millie and Beth closed the big front doors. Millie did one end of the rooms and Beth did the other side. Around 10 pm they were done checking on the guests, and one staff security guard for just The Old Little Plantation Inn walked around the outside of the plantation at night.

Millie got to the room first and sat in one of the chairs and put on the TV. Beth came in and saw her sitting there.

"Do you want to watch a movie before bed?"

Millie got up and walked to their collection and grabbed one of her favorite VHS of My Girl. Millie put the tape in the VHS player. Millie and Beth both got into PJ's, and got in bed and watched the movie together.

Chapter 17

1820

I t was two weeks before Piper and Tyler's one year wedding anniversary. Piper was not the same after Millie was there for a month. Millie had gone back to her time two days before anniversary of Piper's father (Sean Jack Little) had passed away. Tyler did so much for Piper the last two weeks. Piper didn't want to leave baby Jack's room for days after Millie was gone. Piper started going to Sara's old room at night in the hope she would see Millie again.

Tyler wrote a letter to Kitty (Piper's mother) asking her to come and stay with them for a month or so. Tyler hope is that Piper would start acting like herself again. Tyler as went into town to see Lizzie and see if she would come over for lunch 2 times a week. Lizzie said she would love too. Piper was in Jack's room feeding him. Tyler walked in and told Piper that Lizzie was here for lunch. Piper was done feeding baby Jack and put him down for a nap.

Tyler walked Piper down to the dining room and Lizzie was sitting at the table waiting for Piper. Tyler pulls out a chair for Piper. Piper sat down.

"Piper I have some paperwork I need to get done. You and Lizzie can have lunch together."

Tyler left the room. Lizzie and Piper starting talking.

"Lizzie I have something to tell you."

"What is it, Piper."

"Come with me. I have something to show my father and your mother." Piper took Lizzie to Sara's old room. Piper went over to Sara's desk and pulled out a letter that Lizzie's mother wrote to Sean Jack Little. Piper handed the letter to Lizzie.

"Read it." Lizzie looked at the letter than at Piper not know what to do. Lizzie sees that the letter was in her mother's handwriting. Lizzie read the letter.

Lizzie sat on the bed.

"So you and I are sisters?" Piper hugged Lizzie.

"Yes we are half-sisters. I would love for you to move in here with Tyler and I."

Lizzie walked out of the room and down the stairs to the front door.

"Lizzie wait."

Lizzie stop Piper by getting in front of her.

"I am sorry I will give you time to think about this."

Lizzie hugged Piper.

"I will be back tomorrow Piper."

"I will have Tyler pick you up tomorrow."
Lizzie didn't answer Piper back. Lizzie got in her carriage and left the plantation.

Millie

Millie and Beth started planning the holiday event at the end of November. Ben Little was staying at the plantation till the new year in room 20. Millie was in her office that was next to the sitting room. As Millie was in her office work on holiday event the room changed on her. Tyler was in the room talking to Jasper. Tyler looked up and saw her.

"Millie you are back."

Millie didn't know what to say and she was as white as a ghost.

"Millie, you alright?"

Piper came into the room and saw Millie and ran over to hug her. Millie move to the window and didn't want Piper to hug her. Jasper was looking at Millie.

Piper and Tyler walked out of the room, and slowly Millie came out with them. Millie walked out the front doors and sat on a porch chair. Piper sat next to her in the hope that Millie would talk to her.

"Millie it is okay," Piper to her in a low sweet voice.

Millie didn't say a thing to her. Millie was so scared she would be stuck in Piper's timeline again.

With Beth in 2000

Beth went to Millie's office to bring her some lunch. Beth opened the door to see there was no Millie. Beth hope that Millie would be back soon, and not gone like last time. Beth went up to their room to Piper's old trunk to see if there was a note from Millie like last time. Beth found a new notebook in the trunk that had Millie's name on it. Beth open the notebook and saw Millie handwriting and it said.

Millie's Notebook "To my Beth, I am not come back this time. I know you find this notebook after I go back to Piper's time. I have tried to find the "Time Pocket". I have been here now for 3 months. Piper and Tyler and Jasper have helped me get to know this time. I miss you so much. Sometimes I see you walking around the plan-

tation calling out my name. I go to you every time and as soon as I get to you, you're gone again. I am staying in Piper's sister Heather's old room, and I think that is room number 24. Oh my, Beth, I am in hopes that I will make it back to you someday. I will write in this notebook every day so you know I am ok. I love you so much My Beth. Love Always Millie Brown."

Beth went to the store next to their room and looked up anything on Millie at the end of 1820 and the first part of 1821. Beth finds something that she didn't want to see.

In Tyler's notebook, it showed that he and Piper attend the marriage of Millie to Jasper Wood one of Tyler's business partner in 1821. Beth dropped the notebook on the floor and started to cry.

Chapter 18

Millie was back in 1820, and Piper was so happy. Lizzie had moved into Sara's old room, so Piper had Millie in Heather's old room, and Tyler's business partner Jasper Wood staying in their guest house.

It was the start of December and Millie and Jasper had grown close the last month. Piper had a full house again. Her baby boy started talking and moving around the plantation now. Tyler like that he could help his father with the shipping business now that Lizzie and Millie lived at the plantation, and Jasper in the guest house.

Piper knew that one day Millie would be back in her time, but she loved having here with her every day, Lizzie also.

Jasper eyed Millie. Millie was attracted to Jasper, also known had to survive this time period, she had to marry someone.

Piper and Tyler in their room talking about what to do if Millie is to stay longer than 6 months. Piper told Tyler to give it a year before marrying her off to Jasper.

"I will talk to Millie about Jasper wanting to court her."

Piper went to Millie's room and knocked on her door, and Millie opened the door. Piper walked and sat down on the bed.

"Millie I have to let you know that Jasper wants to court you." Millie started laughing.

"Jasper wants to marry me?" still laughing.

"Millie this is not funny. If you are here longer than 6 months you will marry him."
Millie stopped laughing.

"You can't tell me who to marry or make me marry them."

"Millie you are living in my house and I have the right to. I know you are not from this time."

Millie ran out of the room and down the stairs right into Jasper. Jasper grabbed her.

"I hope in a year we will be getting married."

"I know I just heard." Millie walked out the front doors and out to the courtyard. Jasper followed her out there.

"Millie wait,"
Millie stopped.

"What do you want from me, we just met and you want to marry me. You don't know me at all. I am in love with someone else."

Jasper looked at her.

"Who is this man you are in love with?"

Millie wanted to say woman, but knew better.

" He is the city and I am just here for a visit. He and I are getting married after I get back home in a month or so."

Piper came out to the courtyard with Jack in her arms.

Millie walked over to Piper and Jack grabbed at her and she opened her arms to Jack and got in her arms. Piper and Millie walked back to the house.

"I will go tell Tyler about what you just told Jasper."

Piper let Millie take Jack to the sitting room, as she went to talk to Tyler. Millie was playing with Jack in the sitting room. Millie looked up and saw a ghost-like Beth in the sitting room.

"Beth"

Beth didn't see her. Millie got up off the floor and walked to Beth, but she was gone again. Millie cried and Jack pulled on her dress.

"Up."

With his arms out to her. Millie picked him up and took him to his room.

In Jack's room, Millie was playing with him on the floor when Piper came in.

"Moma food."

Piper picked him up and went to her rocking chair. Millie started cleaning up as Piper fed Jack.

"Piper what did Tyler say?"

"He will let Jasper know that he didn't know

about your man. I know you were talking about Beth the woman I saw you with a year ago."

Millie smiled at Beth's name.

"Yes, I was talking about Beth. I know that if I am still here after 6 months. I will marry Jasper or someone you and Tyler pick for me."

"I will let Tyler know so he can tell Jasper. Jasper is a good man, and he will be good to you."

"What will you do if he is not good for me?"

Piper didn't know what to say, because once she marries him, she is his property.

" There is nothing you can do is there?"

"No, you will be his property."

Millie walked out of the room and back to her new room in 1820.

Part Two

Chapter 19

Millie has been living her new life in 1821 in the Little Plantation with her new love Jasper. She had started falling for Jasper after 3 months living in 1821.

Millie had been living at Little Plantation for 6 months now, missing her old life in 2000 and her old love Beth. Millie walked down the stairs and saw Jasper sitting in the sitting room with Tyler. It was the start of summer at "Little Plantation" and it is a month or so away from Jack Little's first birthday. Piper was in the kitchen with Jack feeding him his breakfast.

"Do you want me to help you with Jack today?" Piper looked at Millie.

"Not today, I am starting to feel better with this little one in my belly. You and Jasper should have fun today, while you still can."
Millie hugged her dear friend.

" Do you know something?" Piper smiled at Millie.

"Maybe"

Millie walked back into the sitting room and Tyler got up and went to the kitchen to help his wife. Jasper got up and walked over to Millie in his slow sexy way and made her weak in the knees. Jasper kissed Millie on her cheek and he put his hand into hers and they walked outside. Millie saw her favorite horse being held by one of the hands. Millie walked over to the horse that Jasper had got her over a month ago.

"How is my sweet Lady doing today?"

Lady rubbed on Millie. Lady is a chestnut painted mare.

Jasper walked over to Millie and put his arm around her and kissed her neck. One of the other hands walked over to Jasper with his horse. Jasper helped Millie on her horse and then got on his horse.

Millie and her horse Lady followed Jasper and his horse Mister, a black and white gelding. They had been riding over 10 mins before Jasper stopped and got off his horse Mister and tied Mister to a tree. Jasper walked over to Millie and Lady and helped her down. Millie walked Lady over to Mister and tied her to the same tree.

Jasper walked over to her pick her up and kissed her on the lips with the passion of 20 men. She wrapped her arms around his neck and kissed him back. He put her feet back on the ground.

Jasper whispered his slow sexy voice to her " How would you like to live here?"

Pointed out a large house in the distance. Millie

looked into Jasper's eyes fill with tears in her eyes.

"Love it"

Jasper not knowing that the house in the distance is Millie's home in her time. She kissed him then walked over to Lady and got back on her and rode over to the house.

She got off Lady and tied her to a tree, and she walked up to the door of her childhood house, but the house was so new in 1821. Jasper came in behind her

" Millie my love do you like?"

Spends around looked at Jasper this was the first time he had told her that he loved her. She walked slowly up to him.

"I love you too Jasper."

He smiled at her, then kissed her. They walked into the house and there was nothing in the house yet. She walked up the stairs to her room and it was so new.

" Will we be the first family to live in this house?"

"No this was the old Hall Manor. I helped finish this house a month ago."

They both walked back down stairs and back outside with the horses.

She walked over to Lady just before she got back on her Jasper.

" Millie my love will you marry me?"

Jasper was down on one knee.

" Jasper it would be my honor to be your wife."

Jasper put moonstone engagement rings on Millie's ring finger. He got up off the ground and kissed with love in his heart for her, and she kissed him back love in her for him.

As they got back to The Little Plantation Piper was waiting in the sitting room with young Jack in her lap. Tyler was in his office right next to the sitting room with the door opened. Millie and Jasper walked into the house and Piper got up and ran to Millie.

"Can I see it?"

Millie laughed at Piper and show her the ring. Jasper let the girls have time, as he walked into Tyler's office and closed the door. Piper and Millie walked back to the sitting room and Jack got into Millie's lap and kissed her hand.

Beth 2001

Beth looked in Millie's notebook every day in the hope there would love letter to her again. She saw that Millie had fallen in love with Jasper Wood.

Piper 1821

Piper loved having a full house. Jack First Birthday was in a month and she was pregnant with baby number two, she is six months along. The Little Plantation was doing well, Tyler was working on his shipping business with Jasper. Piper was so happy that Millie and Jasper were getting married and that they would be living just down the street from the Plantation.

Piper has so much planning to do for Jack's birthday party and that her family was going to be staying at the house. She needed to move Millie into the west wing part of the house, since Millie's engagement. She knew that Millie doesn't know that Jasper Wood is one of the wealthiest men in the world.

∞∞∞

Piper and Millie are out in courtyard having lunch while young Jack was having his afternoon nap. Piper looked down at her growing belly and smiled.

" So why are you moving me to the west wing of the house?"

" You need more room to start hire help for your and Jasper's home."

" I don't know how to hire for my house."

"Millie you can have Lizzie help you, and have her as one of your ladies." Millie nodded to Piper just as Lizzie came into the room. Lizzie sat next to Millie and Piper took Jack to his room for a nap.

Chapter 20

Millie

Millie asked Lizzie to be one of her ladies. Lizzie hugged Millie and ran up to her room to start packing up her room. Millie went outside for a walk around and think about her new life she was going to be starting with Jasper. As walked around for about an hour Jasper showed up next to her.

"What are you thinking about Millie?"

Millie looked up at him and gray-blue eyes and kissed him on the lips.

"You and Me"

Jasper kissed her back

" I need to tell you something about my family money."

Millie and Jasper saw a bench next to the Willow tree and they could see their house in the distance.

Jasper told Millie that he is a "Duke in French" and his sister was going to come to New Orleans and be staying at Little Plantation.

"What is her name?"

"Justine and she is 16 years older than me."

Jasper also told her about how his sister had never been married and she also had Damzel Hazel. Millie started laughing as Jasper saying Damzel. Jasper looked at Millie and smiled

"That her name Damzel Hazel, and she has been my sister since I was 2 years old."

Millie hugged Jasper and pulled him off the bench. Jasper walked Millie back to the house.

Millie walks into the sitting room and saw a person she had never seen before. Piper walks up to Millie.

" This is your new teacher Linda Hall"

Linda walked over to Millie and took her hand.

" Miss Millie I am here to teach you Etiquette"

Millie took Linda to her room. Millie's new room at Little Plantation had three rooms. Millie's sitting room was the best place for her studies. Linda sat at the big table puting her books there. Linda looked at Millie and saw something familiar in Millie's eyes.

"What is your mother's name dear?"

Millie had not been asked about her mother since the day she died of breast cancer a month before her 18th birthday.

"Her name was Penelope Brown"

"I knew Penelope Brown 25 years ago, and she married my brother Seth Hall"

"Do you what happend to Penelope and Seth?"

"They had a little girl named Millie Ann Hall, but went Millie was 4 years old my brother was killed in a fight with another man that wanted to be with Penelope."

Linda told Millie that she never saw Penelope and Millie after Millie's 5th birthday party that was here in the Little Plantation on the same day as Piper Little birthday. Millie didn't know what to say to this woman that could be her aunt.

Millie looked at Linda

"I am the Millie you are talking about."

Linda looked at Millie and saw the little girl she knew as a child and hugged her with everything she had and started to cry. Kitty Little came into the room and saw Linda and Millie hugging and crying. Linda looked up at Kitty

"Why didn't you tell me she was alive and well."

Piper and Lizzie came into the room as well.

Millie walked over to Kitty

"You knew my mother and father?"

"Yes I did, Penelope was my best friend"

Piper went over to her mother and hugged her. Kitty looked Piper and cried. Millie looked at her aunt Linda with so much emotion in her eyes. Millie's mother never talked about her father. Millie ran out of the room and didn't stop till she got to her home and ran inside and saw her mother standing there.

"I know why I never told you about your father."

Millie looked at her mother and saw 8 year old Millie watching t.v. Penelope took Millie's hand and led her up the stairs to a small room Millie knew the room well. Penelope told Millie everything she wanted to know about her father Seth Hall. How he was killed by Sean Jack Little, father "Frederick Colin Little."

Millie was at the door after her mother told everything, and saw Jasper standing there looking at her. Millie ran into his arms and cried. Millie hadn't told Jasper her whole story.

" Jasper I need to tell you something about me"

Millie's life story spill out of her with tears in her eyes the whole time. Jasper got closer to her and kissed her head.

" I knew who you were the first time I saw you. Tyler told me all about you and Piper on one trip after falling for you 3 months ago."

Millie looked at him so much love in her eyes to make someone sick. Millie took him into their soon to be room. Millie opened the door and saw the bed in the room.

"Jasper, have you been sleeping here?"

Jasper kissed her, slowly they got into bed and had each other for the first time.

Piper

Piper didn't know what to do about the information about her grandfather and killing Millie's father Seth Hall to be with Millie's mother Penelope. Piper went to young Jack's room and looked at her son as he was sleeping and looked down at her growing belly. Tyler came to Piper hold her so close and whipped in her ear

" I am here for you my love always."

Tyler help his very pregnant wife to bed.

∞∞∞

The next day Piper and her mother Kitty talking about what happened with Millie's mother and father. Millie was not in west wing of the Little Plantation. Piper looked all over the house for Millie.

Piper saw Lizzie outside in the garden with Jack. Piper decded to go out there with her sister and son. Stephen came out to the garden with their lunch. Piper and Lizzie talked to Millie and what had happened the day before.

A short time later after lunch Millie showed up with Jasper. Piper was relieved to see Millie with Jasper. Millie sat next Piper.

" Jasper and I will be getting married in two weeks." Millie stop for second " I'm moving into my house today with Jasper."

Jasper went into the house to Tyler's office.

Piper grabbed at Millie hands.

" I am so sorry for everything. My mother told me everything and how my grandfather killed your father to be with your mother."

Millie hugged Piper. Lizzie got up and started walking to the house to help Millie pack up everything. Millie walked up with Lizzie. Piper sat there with tears rouling down her face and young Jack seeing that his mother was very sad came up to her and hugged and kissed her.

Chapter 21

Millie

I t had been three days since Millie met her aunt and found out about her father Seth Hall. Seeing her mother young and healthy. Millie thought about her and Jasper's first time together. Millie had been with one boyfriend in high school at 16 years old, been with one girlfriend before Beth. Millie thought about Beth for a moment and smiled. The love Millie had for Beth was so different than with Jasper. Jasper's sister Justine and her companion Damzel Hazel were going to be there in two days time.

∞∞∞∞

Millie was enjoying seting up her home with Jasper. Millie and Lizzie got one side of The "Wood Manor" ready for Justine and Damzel Hazel. Jasper had hired some help for the Wood Manor. Millie didn't really know what to do in 1821 the hiring for the house hoed. It was all so new to Millie, being a girl that grew up in the late 20th century.

Justine and Damzel Hazel showed up in style and it was nothing Millie had seen before, that was not in a movie or tv show. The real stuff was way better. Millie had been taking her finishing class so she knew how to greet her guests in the proper way. One of the men Jasper had hire opened big extravagant horse and carriage. Damzel Hazel got out first and helped her Lady out of the carriage. Justine came out of the carriage slowly and looked a lot younger than Millie was thinking. Justine 5'6" Blond hair and piercing sapphire blue eyes. Justine walked right over to Millie and hugged her.

"Thank you".

Millie didn't have a clue what Justine would say Thank you to her for. Justine stepped over to Jasper and kissed him both sides of his cheeks and they hugged.

Millie showed Justine and Damzel Hazel to their side of the house. Millie notices the way Justine looked at Damzel Hazel with a great fire of love for her in Justine's eyes. Millie and Jasper let Justine and Damzel Hazel become well acquainted with their new surroundings before lunch at the Little Plantation.

Jasper and Millie walked down to their part of the house. Jasper looked a little happier.

" I need to tell you about my sister and her companion."

Millie stopped him.
" I see that they are in love with each other,"
Jasper was looking at her
" You are alright with this my love?"
 "Yes, love is love."
Millie told Jasper about Beth and the love she
had for her. Jasper thought about when he first met
Millie and the love she talked about.

∞∞∞∞

Justine and Damzel Hazel clean and are ready
to go to the Little Plantation for lunch. The horse
and carriage perfectly ready to go. Jasper helps all
the ladies in the carriage. It was not a long ride just
being down the street to "The Little Plantation."

Piper

Piper had set up the dining room all ready
for her guests to arrive. Justine got out of the carriage Piper quite surprised beautiful Justine was
for someone who was not married. Justine went
right to up Piper.
 " Little Plantation is breathtaking and so
are you."
 Piper smiled. Tyler came up to Piper with
their son Jack at his side. Justine curtsy to Tyler.
They all walked into the dining room for lunch.
After lunch Piper took young Jack up to his

room for a nap. Millie help Piper.

"You're thought of Justine and Damzel Hazel?"

Piper put sleepy Jack in his bed and walked out into the little sitting-room next to Jack's room and sat down being 7 months pregnant with baby number two. Millie sat next to friend and thanked her for having lunch over here. Piper started to close her eyes.

Chapter 22

Millie

It had been a week since Justine and Damzel Hazel were staying at "The Wood Manor."

Millie finish taking the class with her aunt Linda every day. This was something so new Millie, all really knew growing up was her mother Penelope and this really cool old lady that would pop up from time to time. Millie and Jasper's wedding was the talk of New Orleans. Millie hopes for a small intimate wedding, but Justine wants to go out for her baby brother's big day.

June 30, 1821

Millie at the Little Plantation so Piper, Lizzie, and others could help Millie for the big day. Justine came into Millie's room with French silk purple wedding dress. Everyone in the room gasped at the dress.

The Wedding

Millie walked down the same steps as her mother Penelope did to marry her father Seth

Hall. Jasper asked Tyler to walk his bride down the aisle. Millie loved that Jasper did this for her. Tyler and Millie didn't tell Jasper that she had asked Tyler right after they got engaged on June 1. Tyler got to Millie's door and opened into find Millie looking out the window at the Wood Manor. Tyler asked

"Millie are you ready to do this." Millie looked at Tyler
"Yes"
Millie walked down the steps to Jasper and looked in his eyes with so much love for her. Millie and Tyler walked down the steps. All eyes on Millie, but she just saw Jasper. Time stop, Millie saw her mother and father getting married.

"Millie," Tyler said and grabbed her.
Millie had tears in her eyes. Millie started walking again down the aisle to Jasper. Jasper took Millie's hand and kissed it with sweet and loving . Millie and Jasper's wedding ceremony was everything and more for both of them.

Millie and Jasper wedding reception was at The Wood Manor with their yard roses, sunflowers and lavender. Millie and Jasper's reception was short and sweet.

∞∞∞

July 3 1821 Millie was over the moon.

The Wood Manor was coming along quite nicely. In a weeks time Justine and Damzel Hazel were going back home French. Millie Told Jasper all about seeing her mother and father on their wedding day. First time Millie just saw the past and got stuck there with no way back. Millie was so happy being in her new life in 1821.

Chapter 23

Beth 2001

Beth had moved on from Millie Beth still worked at the Old Little Plantation. Ben Little hand-picked Beth The GM. Old Little Plantation was no longer Inn.

Millie notebooks for Beth. Millie telling Beth were the Deed of The Wood Manor and signed a letter from Millie so that Beth could live at the Wood Manor and take care of the place. Beth moved into the wood manon and saw the old family portrait of Millie and her family. Beth went right up to it then it was gone, and everything in the room was like new.

A forty-five year oldMillie looking right at her.

"Beth my dear one do you want to go back to your time? I know how to get you back there now."

Beth nodded at Millie and took Beth's hand and helped Beth to her time and place. Millie hugged Beth then Millie was gone again.

Beth picks up the Millie notebooks from 1845. Millie left her a little note.

"Beth it was great seeing you again. I see you have moved into my home. Thank you for what you are going to do for me the same day. Your friend in Time Millie Ann Hall Wood."

Piper

July 30 1821 Jack's birthday was today and Piper was 8 months pregnant. Piper wanted to do a small party for her Jack. Dean and wife Emily and their son. Kitty and Heather and her Wesley and Lizzie. Piper had not seen much of Millie and Jasper since their wedding day. Piper remembers how fun and enjoyable her and Tyler's first month together were. Lizzie had moved back to the Little Plantation to help Piper more with Jack.

Young Jack walked down the big Plantation steps with his daddy Tyler holding his hand. Jack and Tyler in their formal wear. Piper blissful at seeing her Son and Husband. Tyler got to Piper

" I will finish up"

Lizzie helped Piper to her room and helped dress Piper in the new teal dress Tyler got her.

Piper walked outside in the grand and saw everyone she loved there. Millie walked over to her and hugged

" You are glowing and I am with child."

Piper started to cry as she did so did Millie.

The staff at the Little Plantation brought out the entrees for Jack on his first birthday. Piper was just so happy having full house again. Piper wanted to know if her mother Kitty would move back home with her and the kids. Piper did have dry nurse and nanny, but still, she wanted her mother with her. Millie being with child Piper needed to help Tyler with Plantation business, so Tyler could work more on his shipping business.

Jack Little's party was over and Piper looking at Tyler then their son. Jack had fallen asleep on a wooden swing that his daddy had made for him. Tyler walked over to his son and picked Jack up took him to his room.

Piper, Millie both sat on the wooden swing. Piper saw the shine in Millie's eyes.

"How are you feeling?"

while grinning from ear to ear.

"Overjoyed over the moon."

Both Piper and Millie giggle.

Part 3

Piper May Little and Tyler Christopher Williams

Family Tree

Jack Tom Little Williams 1820

Marie Sara Little Williams 1821

Gasper Sean Little Williams 1824

Twin Girls

Wendy May Little Williams 1825

Opal Rae Little Williams 1825

Hallie Lizzie Little Williams 1827

Owen Tyler Little Williams 1828

Millie Ann Hall Wood and Jasper Sawyer Wood

Family Tree

Twin

Allie Penny Hall Wood 1822

Justin Peter Hall Wood 1822

Hannah May Hall Wood 1823

Twin Boys

Sawyer Jasper Hall Wood 1824

Willow Tree Hall Wood 1824

Lucy Sallie Rose Hall Wood 1826

Chapter 24

Allie

F ull moon in the night sky on March 26 1841 on Millie and Jasper twins Justin and Allie 19th birthday. Allie was the older twin. Tonight was Allie being introduced into society.

Allie knew who she wanted to marry and that was Jack Little William, Piper and Tyler's oldest son. Allie had been in love with Jack since she was 16. Jack saw Allie like a sister in way, Allie was only 8 months younger than Jack's sister Marie. Allie and Marie are the best friends.

Marie had her big party on her 19th birthday and was starting to see young men from her for the past 6 months. Allie was happy for her friend but knew as well that Marie would marry him and move out of the Little Plantation.

The Plantation would go to Jack and his lady of choice. Allie so wished for it to be her.

Allie party

Millie helps her Allie get ready for her night. Jasper and Justine down in The Wood Maron small ballroom. Jasper wants the best of the best for his Allie tonight. Allie dress was made from the best french silk and it was pale lavender. Millie and Jasper wanted to give their Allie a chance to pick her suitor. Jasper came up and got Allie. Allie walked in with her father on her arm. All eyes on were Allie as she was a stunningly beautiful young woman. Allie looked all over for Jack, but couldn't find him. One by one young men would ask her to dance.

Jack

As Allie comes into the room, time stoped for Jack. This was the first time he had ever see Allie look so eye-opening amazing that he had to leave the room. Piper came up to her son

"Allie looks beautiful"

Jack was red in the face.

Piper looked at Jack and knew he had true feelings for Allie. Piper and Millie joke at the way Jack would be at Allie's side. Piper made Jack go back to the ballroom.

"Looks like Allie needs a break from all her suitor"

Jack looked at Allie and saw the look on her face help me, Jack. Jack walked over to Allie and the guy dancing with her.

"may I have this dance, Allie?"

Allie let go of the guy and went right into Jack.

"Thank you".

Jack took Allie out to the Wood Maron gazebo. Jack was taller than Allie. Jack looked down at her and said very sweetly

" We can stay out here all night if you want to with me?"

Allie looked up and hugged him and as she letting him go Jack kissed her on the lips so very soft tender.

Millie

Millie walked over to Piper to see if she knew where Allie was. Piper pointed outside Millie saw Jack and Allie kissing.

" I told you Jack would see my Allie tonight."

"Let them have this first moment together."

Millie and Piper walked back in the house.

Jasper walked over to his wife and the mother of his 6 children. Hannah their second daughter who was almost 18 years old walked over to her mother and father, right behind her was Sawyer and Willow the identical twin boys of Millie and Jasper. Sawyer and Willow 16 years old, and after them was Lucy the baby of the family at the age of 15 years old.

Allie and Jack came back into the house, and like Jack's mother and father 22 years age all eyes were on Allie and Jack.

Piper

Piper could feel her Jack wanting everyone to stop looking at him and Allie. Piper told Tyler to get Jack for her. Jack walked over to his mother red in the face.

" Jack my dear is Allie the one for you?"

He looked at his mother little boy eyes and in a deep voice

"Yes, she the one for me. She always has been."

With big lovesick grin on his face and he went back to Allie's side. Piper so happy that Jack was in love with the girl down the street.

Chapter 25

Hannah

Hannah and sisters are very close, but never really thought this was the time for her to be in. Millie hadn't told her kids that she grew up in the late 20th century. Two weeks after Allie's party Hannah doesn't see her sister as much as they did before everything changed with Allie and Jack. Hannah's 18th birthday was on May 17, and she didn't want a party like Allie and Lucy do. Hannah was out in the gazebo with Justin, Sawyer, and Willow.

Allie and Jack

Allie and Jack are Twin Flames. Jack at 5 started telling his mother I need to see Allie every day. Millie would show up with Allie and he never left her side. At 10 Allie started to have real feelings for Jack.

Jack 12 was not into having a girl as a friend.

So Millie and Piper told Allie to give him time to see you, my dear. Allie did that until she was 14 almost 15. One of Jack's good friends Chester started looking at Allie in the way she wanted Jack too. Jack at 18 started seeing Allie's true light of beauty, but she was seeing his good friend Chester. Allie and Chester stop seeing each other 3 months ago.

Millie

Millie noticed went she was pregnant with Allie and Justin she could see and find the "Time Pocket" in both Little Plantation and Wood Manor. Millie hadn't told her children of her past. It was the day after her Allie party. Millie walked over to the little plantation to talk to Piper about their kids getting married. Millie was almost there when she saw Beth walk to her.

"Beth"

Beth looked up and saw Millie.

Millie walked right into the Time Pocket Beth looked at Millie.

" It's been a long time my friend you still just as lovely even more than last time I saw you in 2000 and saw a little older you in 2001."

Millie just hugged her friend. Millie walked out of the Time Pocket and saw Piper looking at her.

"I just saw Beth, Piper."

Piper walked over to Millie and they walked

over to the wooden swing and sat down.

Piper

Piper didn't know that Millie could still go in the "Time Pocket" like she did.

"Millie is the first time you have since Beth?"

Millie looked down and said in saded voice

"No. I have seen her off and on for the past 20 years. I see and find here and at my home. After I got pregnant with Allie and Justin and all of my pregnancies."

Piper saw Jack and Allie coming out of the house and they walked over to their mothers. Jack got a chair for Allie and she sat down and looked at Piper.

" Jack and I talked aboutn't and we want to wait a year before we get married, so we can get to know each other in this new found love for each other now."

Piper wanted this for her son and Allie. Piper had wished her parents had done this with her and Tyler after they met at that town meeting. Piper got up and hugged Allie then her son Jack and whisper in Jack ear

"I am proud of the man you are becoming"

Piper kissed and sat back down next Millie. Allie and Jack walked away from their mothers to their spot in the Little Plantation garden. Piper's second son Gasper at 16 years old walked over to his mother.

" Mom I am going to help father on the ship next week for a month." Gasper walked over to the horse barn for his daily ride on his horse. Fifteen-year-old Wendy and Opal twins girls of Piper and Tyler playing around Jack and Allie. Thirteen-year-old Hallie and twelve Owen walked over to their father Tyler on the porch.

Chapter 26

Jack and Allie

I t was the start of Autumn last September and Allie wants to be with Jack. Allie had it all planned out as did Jack. Their love blossomed so much in the past 6 months. Allie and Jack wanted to go out for their daily walk around stream behind The Wood Manor.

The cold air and the way colors of tree changed, just as they had together. Jack loves Allie with a passion fire inside him could not take any more. Jack kissed Allie in the way he had never done before. Allie so rosy from the kiss. Allie kissed Jack back.

They both on the grand embracing each other. Jack stopped himself before he took his Allie.

" What is it, Jack?"

"Marry me tonight?"

"YES"

They both got up and ran to the Wood Manor and saw Millie and Jasper.

"Mother and Father Jack and I want to get married tonight."

Millie got up and took Allie up to Allie's room. Jack ran out of the house and to his home, as he came into the sitting room.

"Father and Mother Allie and I are getting married tonight."

Tyler walked over to his son and took him to the west wing.

Piper

Piper and Lizzie started setting up for Jack and Allie Wedding in 3 hours. It was around 3 clock went Jack came into the sitting room to tell everyone that Allie and him getting married tonight. Marie, Wendy, Opal, and Hallie help get things ready.

Piper went over to the Wood Manor to help Millie with Allie. Piper walked up to Allie's room and saw that Allie's wedding dress was a lot like her wedding dress. Allie dress was teal with pale lavender sash.

Millie

Millie didn't see Piper come in the room.

"Allie who are looking at?"

"She's looking at me."

Millie saw her best friend in this world looking at her Allie and time stopped.

Millie saw her mother in the Time Pocket and

she blow Millie a kiss in the air.

"Mom"

Millie saw her Allie again.

"Who was that woman?"

Millie looked at Allie.

"That was my mommy in the year 1998 just before she dies."

"1998?"

Millie sat her Allie down and told her everything as Hannah came in the door. As Hannah came in Piper went back to get herself ready for her and Tyler Jack's wedding to Allie. Millie walked over to her Hannah.

"You need to know also."

Millie's life spills out her like a book. Both Allie and Hannah

"Does father know this about you?"

"Yes he does and everything I am telling you both right now."

Millie finnished her life story to her girls.

"Allie my dear this is your night with Jack. I think we should talk more about this soon."

Millie kissed both of her girls and helped Allie up.

Jack and Allie Wedding

In the Wood Manor gazebo, a small group of family and friends are waiting to see Jack and Allie get married. Jack was in the same spot where he had kissed Allie for the first time. Jasper walked his little girl right to Jack. Allie walks right next to Jack. Tyler performs a ceremony for Jack and Allie. Time stopped for Allie and Jack, till they both hear.

" You may kiss your bride"

Jack looked down at Allie and kissed the same way he did when they kissed for the first time.

Chapter 27

Hannah

Hannah knew she was like aunt Justine, and her mother told more about her life before meeting and fell in love with their father. Millie had told Hannah all about Beth and living in the late 20th century.

Hannah wants to tell her mother that she wanted to live in the 21st century, so she could find herself. Hannah had it set to tell her mother. Allie came in the house looking for their mother.

"Hannah. I have to tell someone. I am with child."

Allie and Jack married for almost a year. Hannah hugged her sister. Hannah was the only one that knew Allie had lost her first baby. Hannah looked at her big sister and said with love

"Do you want to tell mother."

Allie noped. Hannah walked with her sister to Wood Maron garden and as they walked Allie and Hannah both saw old and new.

Millie saw her girls going in and out of "Time Pocket" as she did. Hannah saw her mother and then saw a stirring woman and with 10-year-old boy waving at her. Hannah complete draw into the woman and the boy and Allie was gone. The young boy ran up to her.

"Mommy"

As Hannah stop looked around to see her mother looking at her and the woman and the boy were gone.

Millie

Millie knew what was going on, she saw the little boy also.

"Mama I have to tell you I am with child."

Millie looked at Allie and started crying. Millie hugged her Allie. Millie was over the moon by the news.

Both girls helped their mother harvesting the vegetables for the week. After they were done went in the house. Jasper was in the sitting room. Allie hugged her father and said little girl like

" I'm with child papa."

Pure joy on his face and kissed his first little girl forehead than walked over to Millie kissed her and picked her up off the ground. Millie and Jasper walked to the pantry Allie and Hannah handed their mother and father the vegetables and went up to Hannah's room.

Shortly after the girls left the room Millie

told Jasper about what she saw, Beth and Hannah saw a woman and 10-year boy.

"I think are Hannah is meant to be in the 21st century."

Jasper looked so sad at Millie had said to him, about him Hannah.

"Hannah is like your sister"

Jasper knew this was true about Hannah.

"She can have a good life in the 21st century free to love whoever she wants, and have the life she needs to stay here in the world," Millie add to Jasper.

Piper

Piper was working paperwork on the Little Plantation while Tyler was in town with Jack. Lizzie came into the room.

"Si Tyler and Si Jack are home."

Piper got up and went down the stairs to see her son caring a bassinet up to the west wind. Jack looked up to see his mother

"We are with child mother."

Tyler came up to Piper and kissed her.

Allie came walking up the stairs to the west wind. Piper ran to Allie and hugged and kissed.

"You are going, to be a great mother."

Allie started to cry.

"I just hope this one will stay with me."

Piper looked at Allie and knew what Allie was talking about. Piper had lost a baby boy after the twins.

"Come here my girl"

Piper told Allie all about losing her baby boy.

Chapter 28

Allie and Jack

It had been 6 months since the news of Jack and Allie's little one. Allie was 8 months with child.

The west wind of the Little Plantation and saw all Time Pocket.

One day Allie saw younger Millie with Piper old trunk and said something to Jack and went into the Time Pocket. Jack came back to Allie.

"Why did you do that?"

Jack looking at his pregnant wife.

" Something inside told me to do it that way."

A 45-year-old Millie walked up to Jack and laughed at him.

"Now I know why you did that to me all those years ago."

Allie looked at her mother.

" Hannah made a decision?"

"She will be over for dinner tonight to let all of us know."

Allie went up to her and Jack's room for a nap.

Hannah

Hannah came over to Little Plantation for dinner with her sister and all the people she loved in this world. Hannah wanted to live in the 21st century, but she wanted to wait for Allie to have her and Jack's child. Hannah walked into the dining room and the room change on her and she saw the woman again, but she was around the same age as Hannah.

" What is year and what is your name?"

" My name is Violet and the year is 2025. Are you one of the new girls that Miss Beth just hired?"

"Yes I am, and my name is Hannah May Hall Wood"

" That quite a name."

Hannah got hot and red in the face.

Violet showed Hannah Beth's office as Hannah walked with Violet the room changed on her.

"Hannah."

Hannah looked at her mother and started to cry.

"I saw her too as did Allie, do you want to go back and be with her?"

"I want to wait to untie Allie has the little one."

Allie came over to her sister and hugged.

" Dear Hannah go live your life in that time."

Hannah sat down at the table and started eating the food.

Beth 2025

Violet came in Beth's office

"Hannah"

"Who's Hannah?"

"Hannah May Hall Wood one the new girls you hired"

"I have no Hannah May Hall Wood on my list"

Beth knows that name from Millie Ann Brown Hall Wood notebooks to Beth. Beth took Violet to the Little Plantation library and showed photos of Allie and Jack's wedding. Violet at old photos and saw Hannah.

"How can this be?"

Beth sat poor Violet down and told her about Millie and Piper.

Millie 1845

Millie and Piper sat in their spot at the Little Plantation. Millie knowing far too well what her dear Hannah was going through at this time. Millie knew she had to go through one of the Time Pockets and talk to Beth.

Piper wanted to go with her. Both Millie and Piper talked the halls of little plantation to see or feel the Time Pocket. They got to Jack's old nursery and Millie started to feel the room change, and there was Beth with Violet looking at old photos. Beth looked up and saw Millie and Piper. Poor Violet didn't know what to do. Millie walked over to Beth and hugged her.

" Can we talk to you about my Hannah?"

Beth asked Violet to leave the room. Millie sat down

"My Hannah wants to live in this time. Can you watch over her for me?"

"I can do that for you, my friend, in time."

Millie got up hugged Beth.

"thank you"

Millie walked back to Piper and they walked back into their time.

Piper

Piper hugged Millie as she went back home to her family. Jack came up to his mother.

" Allie needs your help mother"

Piper walked over to Jack and Allie's room to see Allie in the bed crying.

" Hannah is beautiful"

Piper walked over to Allie and hugged her.

As Piper hugged Allie   Millie came into the room. Piper looked up at Millie and

" Allie saw Hannah older and with her son."

Millie and Piper told Allie about all the times

they saw each other in the Time Pocket.

Chapter 29

Hannah

Hannah was torn about leaving or staying with her family. Hannah saw Violet two more times one at Little Plantation and Wood Maron. Hannah was in her room went the room change on her and she saw the 10-year-old boy again.

"Mommy you are so young."

"I am your mom? What is your name sweety?"

"Eric mama."

Violet walk into the room and saw younger Hallie sitting there.

"Hannah my love I will see you again soon."

Violet and Eric were gone.

Hannah got up off her bed and walked down to the sitting room to see her mother. Hannah told Millie about seeing the little boy again and his name is Eric, Violet. Hannah sat down next to her mother.

"Hannah my dear do you want to go there and stay?"

"I think I need too."

Millie got up took Hannah by the hand and walked her around the house and saw younger Violet with Beth and Ben next to the older portrait of the Wood family.

"Hannah, do you feel that change in the air right there?"

Hannah looked at the spot her mother point at and saw Violet and walked to her. Millie let her daughter go to her new life in 2025.

Hannah walked over to Violet. Ben stopped Hannah.

" Great Great Aunt Hannah. I am one Allie and Jack's great-great-grandson."

Hannah hugged him with everything she had.

" Allie child will live, and you are the great proof of that."

Hannah let Ben go and walked right up to Violet. Violet was so red in the face and she could't believe Hannah was really here in her time.

Millie

Jasper came to Millie.

" What is it, Millie?"

"I helped Hannah to time that she needed to be in. Just I did 20 years ago."

Jasper kissed Millie and then walked her over

to the Little Plantation.

Millie and Jasper almost to the Little Plantation

"Mother and Father." Hannah around her 30 with her 10-year-old son Eric. Millie stopped as did Jasper, Hannah hugged them both as did Eric.

Hannah told Millie about Ben. Millie just smiled.

" That why he was so cool with me popping in and out of Time Pocket for a year."

Hannah walked Eric around them and were gone. This was Jasper's first time in Time Pocket. Millie looked at him and kissed him on the cheek.

" Jasper see, she will be just fine."

"I know she will be, I will miss her"

They walked up to the Little Plantation house and saw Allie in the sitting room with Piper. Jasper needed to talk to Tyler and let the ladies have their time together. Mille looked at her Allie knowing who Ben was to her, Allie, and Piper. Allie to Millie

"I know she is gone to her right time with Violet and Eric"

Allie looked down at her growing belly.

"Mother sit with me and feel him kick me."

Allie put Millie's hand on her belly.

"Hannah told me about the man my son will be in this world and his children and Ben to you."

Chapter 30

Allie and Jack

Allie and Jack's son Ben was 6 months old now. Allie missed her sister every day, but she was so happy with her Little family. Lucy had moved to France to help aunt Justine and to take over the palace after she passed away. Lucy wrote Allie a letter every month.

Lucy's letter for this month

" My Dear Sister,

     Life here at the palace, aunt Justine is not doing well after Damzel Hazel passed away two weeks ago. I'm helping the best I can. I miss you and Hannah every day. I have a new gentleman caller. His name is Leodegrance and I know he is the one for me and I to him. More soon my dear sister Love from you little sister Lucy Sallie Rose Hall Wood"

     Allie looked at Jack with their son Ben in the west wind sitting room.

"Jack looks like Lucy is in love again we will see if this one will really be one. I think he is number 3 to be the one for her."

Millie came into the room with a letter from Lucy also.

" That poor boy not knowing what is in store for him with our Lucy."

Jack walked over with baby Ben to his grandma.

"Allie I needed to go and help our father with the work at the shipyard."

Jack kissed his wife and went to work.

Millie

Millie looked at her grandson with more love than she had ever felt before.

"Allie my dear would like for me to stay here with her while Jack is at sea with Tyler and our father?"

" Mama I will be fine, they will just be gone for 3 months."

Millie is so proud of how her Allie's in this moment. Millie let Allie have her time with her son Ben. Millie got to the sitting room and saw Piper. Millie knew Piper didn't like Tyler and Jack were going to be gone for 3 months.

"Piper everything will be just fine."

Piper looked up at her dear friend smiled.

Part 4

Chapter 31

Piper

L ate afternoon on April 17 1850 on Tyler's birthday, and Piper was in their room looking out the window in hope that Jack and Tyler are safe and will be home soon.

"Piper"

Piper looked around to see a 19-year-old Millie.

Piper had tears in her eyes.

"So young my Millie"

"What going on Piper, why so sad?"

"My Tyler and Jack are lost at sea."

Piper knew this Millie would tell her about what happened to Tyler and Jack. Millie asked Piper do you want to know their what destiny is? 19-year-old Millie said they will be back tomorrow. Piper hugged 19-year-old Millie.

"Thank you so much"

Younger Millie was gone, as a 49-year-old Millie come into the room.

Piper ran to her good friend and hugged her.

" They will all be home tomorrow."

Millie looked and saw a Time Pocket on the bed, remember telling Piper about Tyler and Jack being just fine and home tomorrow, but couldn't recall if Jasper was alive or dead. Piper notice how pale Millie was.

"Do you what happens to your Jasper?"

"No. I know 5 of the men died, but I do not know about Jasper."

The next day Piper and Allie knew that their loves would be home. Piper sat with almost 5-year-old Ben, and 3-year-old Ruby. Piper knew Millie looking for Time Pocket so she would know what happen to her Jasper.

Outside Piper could hear Tyler, Jack and Jasper talking, she got up with both kids in her arms. Jack saw his kids and ran to them both and kissed them.

"Papa is never leaving you three again."

"The four of us"

Allie hugged and kissed Jack. Piper and Tyler kissed.

Millie

Millie walked out of the house and saw Jasper run to her and kissed fire in his heart for Millie. Millie started to cry.

" I didn't know if you were dead or alive, younger me didn't know about you yet, but I knew Tyler and Jack."

Jasper kissed her again

"I will always come home to you."

Millie and Jasper hugged Allie and the grand-kids and walked home. Justin and his wife Lillian had been staying with Millie while after hearing that his father was lost at sea. Justin family two boys Barry 4 years old, and Cawley 2 years old. Lillian hugged her father-in-law then Millie. Justin started packing up for his family trip home.

Chapter 32

Hannah 2030

Hannah had been loving and living in the 21 century for 5 years now. Hannah and Violet had adopted their son Eric four years ago when he was one year old. Hannah got her GED right after she came in this Time Pocket to be with Violet.

Hannah was studying to be a history teacher, after all, she was born in 1823 and lived 1800's for 22 years. Hannah opened up the Wood Manor to the public two years ago. She wanted people to know about The Wood family.

Both Allie and her mother wrote notebooks for her to know everything that was going on in their lives.

Beth came like a mother to Hannah. Ben and his Little family called Hannah

"Auntie Hannah"

Hannah loved it. One of Ben's granddaughters was so much like Allie, very which was comforting to Hannah. It was like she never lost her sister in time. Catie is 23 years old.

Hannah starting reading Allie's notebook from 1850, and every notebook started the same with

"My dear sister in time. I am with child again I am hoping for a girl so Ruby can have a sister. I miss you and Lucy. Lucy and Leodergrance are finally getting married after three whole years together. I almost lost my Jack to the sea. Jack is staying with Little Plantation and not the ship work like his father. Father is safe as well dear sister."

Hannah read more of Allie notebooks.

Allie and Jack 1855

It had been five years since Jack decided to take over The Little Plantation from his mother Piper. Jack and Allie moved into the bigger part of the house. Piper and Tyler still stayed in the room.

Jack's sibling Maire married with 6 kids lived across town. Gasper moved to California to be part of the Gold Rush and still not married. The twins Wendy and Opal started working at Lizzie's fabric shop. Hallie and her husband moved to New York City with their three boys. Owen and his wife stayed at the Little Plantation guesthouse with three girls.

Allie's sibling twins brother Sawyer and Willow followed Gasper to the California Gold Rush. Willow got married, but not Sawyer.

Allie and Jack's last child was a girl named Beatrice from Allies' favorite William Shakespeare play "Much Ado About Nothing".

Millie

Millie knowing the outcome of events of the American Civil War that would start in 6 years, and that the southern states would not win in the end. Millie kept this big secret from all she loved. Millie not sure if she would change the history she knows from her past in the 1990's.

Jasper enjoyed having Millie all to himself for the first time in their life together. Millie's joyful that Jasper is aging like fine french wine, and his eyes peak of blue middle of rainstorm still has the young man look.

Chapter 33

Piper

Piper stayed in her and Tyler's room after Tyler died a week ago. It was August 3 1860 Millie knocked on Piper's door.

" Piper open the door."

Piper got of their bed and opened the door for Millie to came in. Piper went right back to their bed and started to cry.

Millie hugged her friend. Jack came into the room with a box for his mother, with Tyler's handwriting on the box.

"Happy birthday my love my life"

Piper opened the box and saw all journals Tyler had written about their love story. Piper put up the first journal and it revealed a note from Tyler from last month.

"My Stunningly beautiful wife and mother of our 7 amazing children. I ask Jack to give you my journal about our love. Love you always your Tyler."

Millie started to leave the room as Piper stopped her from leaving.

"Please stay with me my dear friend"

In a low sad voice. Millie stayed with Piper till she fell asleep.

Millie

Slowly came out of Piper and saw the room change on her and saw a 12-year-old Piper.

"Piper it is Millie."

The 12-year-old Piper hugged Millie.

"You are so old Millie"

"I am my dear Piper I am in my 40's"

Millie knew that Piper said that she was in her 40's, even though Millie is 60 years old.

Millie told young Piper to write in a notebook every time they met in the "Time Pocket"

Millie saw the Time Pocket back to the time she was from and walked into it and saw Allie. Millie hugged Allie. Millie stayed in the west wing for the night. Millie walked into the room to see Jasper in bed waiting for her.

"I knew you would not leave Piper so I moved some of our stuff back to the west wind. Justin, Lillian, and kids are going to move into the Wood Maron. So you and I help Piper."

Millie got into bed with Jasper and went right to sleep.

Hannah 2035

Hannah had read almost all of Millie's notebooks, Allie's notebooks, and Piper's notebooks.

Hannah started looking at Tyler's journals

and looked at the Little note for Piper and seeing that Tyler died a week before her mother and
Piper's birthday on August 3, 1860.

It was August 3 2035 and Old Little Plantation always had reenactment of Piper coming out
party and the night Tyler asked her to marry him.
Hannah knowing as well Beth, and Ben knowing
that was the start of the Time Pocket for her
mother Millie.

Hannah knew that her father would almost a
year later in 1861.

Hannah's older brother Justin died in the American civil war at the battle of Gettysburg on July 1
1863 at the age of 41, and his wife Lillian remar-
ried.

Hannah's twin brothers Sawyer and Willow
had moved to San Diego,Ca in 1860, Willow and
his wife had 10 kids together. Sawyer never got
married. Willow and Sawyer both died on the
same day in 1890 at the age of 66.

Lucy wrote books about her "Adventure of
being the Duchess Apprentice." Lucy did married
Leodergrance and they had 2 girls and 2 boys.

Jack had died in 1888 and Allie moved back
to the Wood Maron. Allie lived to be 90 years old.

Her mother Millie lived to be 80 years old, on
her and Piper's birthday August 3, 1880.

Piper 1880

Mist lingered over the property Little Plantation on the outskirts of New Orleans, just as it had on Piper's 19th birthday.

The whole day 80-year-old Piper stay in her room. It had been 20 years without her Tyler and been one month without her dear friend Millie. Piper desperately wanted to see her friend again.

The sun was setting and Piper hear Millie's voice, but it sounded so young.

"Millie is that you?"

Piper saw a 19-year-old Millie looking at her. Millie.

"Yes, who is in here?"

Piper walked into the light.

"I am Piper Little"

"Piper. Piper, you are in the year 1999."

Piper was not believing Millie.

"No, you are in the year 1880."

Piper watched as Millie put the light on in Piper's room. Piper looked up a saw 1990's light over her bed. Piper.

    "I am in your time."

    " Yes, you are."

Millie sat next Piper on her bed. Piper looked at her dear friend so young and full of life.

    "Millie I miss you, my old friend."

After Piper said this to 19-year-old Millie she was gone again. Piper looked at Time Pocket and saw her Tyler and Millie coming to take her home.

The End

About The Author

Erin Marie Pero grew up in the east part of San Diego County, with her two older sister and her mom and dad. Erin was in special education classes for learning disabilities in spelling and grammar and others. Her form being a passion foe stories and jotted them down. Erin worte a lot of short stories more than she recalled. Now Erin Marie Courtney and still lives in her hometown of San Diego County, with her husband and their three cats and one dog.

Made in the USA
Middletown, DE
24 July 2021

44527226R00102